THE COWBOY SONGWRITER'S FAKE MARRAIGE

THE BRIDES WANTED MATCHMAKER SERIES

LUCY MCCONNELL

THE COWBOY SONGWRITER'S FAKE MARRIAGE

Advertising for a wife is crazy…
But it might just work…
A marriage of convenience is Xavier's last-ditch effort to salvage his career as a
songwriter. He doesn't believe true love strikes twice in a lifetime, but he needs a
coparent and best friend.
When Emily says "I do," he questions his ability to remain neutral in the
marriage.
She's more than he hoped for…
And everything he feared…
Can Xavier give himself over to the experience of loving again? Or, will he shut
away his heart?

You'll love this contemporary romance because every heart longs to find
its match.

CLAIM YOUR FREE BOOK TODAY!

An *It Could Happen to You* retelling with a twist!

This story is an irresistible contemporary romance about a not-so-humble cop who splits his raffle ticket with an unlucky waitress and the actor who falls in love with her.

You'll also be registered for Lucy's newsletter where you'll receive free delicious recipes and updates about her book releases.

Go to:
https://mybookcave.com/d/c7300449/
to receive your FREE gift.

1

XAVIER

*W*hen he became a father, Xavier Cohen had dreams of singing songs around the campfire, Christmas mornings full of wrapping paper and giggles, and building pillow forts in the front room. He hadn't pictured holding his three-day-old baby as they lowered his wife's casket into the ground. He hadn't thought about the endless nights of diaper changes and bottle feedings. The knowledge of how empty a house could feel on the first day of school hadn't been a part of his life.

And yet, he'd done all those things and more.

So why was it so hard to hear the doctor say things like *your son is overweight; he's prediabetic* and *you need to teach Cody healthier habits?* These were hard things to hear, but he'd been through worse. Gathering himself and his son, he thanked the pediatrician and promised to make the needed changes. They'd be back in six weeks for another checkup.

He drove through Moose Creek in a brain fog. The small shops on Main blurred in his peripheral vision. The Jade Mountain range to the west looked like a watercolor painting done in blues, greens, and browns.

Cody watched a movie on Xavier's phone in the back seat. He wore his racecar pajamas, and his hair was a mess. He'd not felt good when they rolled out of bed this morning, and his skin had been sallow. Frightened, Xavier had rushed him into the doctor without getting him dressed. He glanced down at his own plaid pajama pants and then at the clock. It was well after noon.

Xavier couldn't seem to wrap his brain around the type 2 diagnosis. He stared hard out the windshield, willing his mind to get in the game, only to find emptiness where there should have been decision.

Instead of waking up to handle the situation, another thought came in—one that was equally disturbing. He'd been in a state of survival for seven years. He couldn't move forward, and he hadn't the energy to face the past. He got through each day and the fog allowed him to function; at the same time, it held him captive and prevented him from writing songs.

He pulled into the driveway to find Mark's car idling. Crap! He and his agent were supposed to meet at eleven-thirty. He was a half hour late. He jumped out of the car. "Hey." He jogged over to Mark's door and tapped on the window. "Sorry. I had to take Cody to the doctor. You want to come in?" He might have been embarrassed about running around in his pajamas in front of his agent, but he'd known Mark since college and they were friends first.

Mark rolled the window down and pulled off his aviators. "Is he contagious?"

"No." He didn't feel like going into the whole diabetes thing right now. He was barely hanging on as a songwriter; he didn't want his buddy to know how much he failed as a father. And maybe it wasn't so much a failure on his part, but it sure felt that way.

Cody had climbed out of the car and made his way through the front door without saying hello to their guest. He moved like he had on a wet coat. Was that the diabetes? The doc had covered the basic symptoms and Mark checked them off one by one. He should have been more aware of what was happening with his kid, but he thought kids had to go the bathroom a lot. Apparently, not as much as Cody had been. He didn't know how he was supposed to know these things, but he should have.

"Let's do this." Mark rolled the window up. His car was new, silver and shiny. He wore a navy suit and a thin tie. His hair was longer than it had been six months ago but styled.

"You've gone Hollywood," Xavier teased. He led the way up the steps to the front door. Mark had started his career selling Xavier's music. He had clients that sold songs to some of the biggest names in country music. He might have started small, but he'd made a big splash.

They entered, and Mark tripped over a remote-control car in the entranceway. He paused, his hand on the wall for balance. "You've gone single-male disaster."

Xavier looked around the room, seeing it through Mark's eyes. He couldn't remember the last time he'd actually looked at his house. There were toys spread from one wall to the other, littering the carpet and creating death traps. Some of them were for toddlers. He should have donated the lot ages ago. The couch was covered in half-empty chip bags and candy wrappers. The recycle bin overflowed with soda cans. Pizza boxes stacked next to the garage door. Clothes were pretty much everywhere.

Mark put his hand on Xavier's shoulder. "You're getting worse, not better, bro."

Xavier scrubbed his face, noting the week's worth of hair on his chin. "It's only this bad because Cody's out of school. Our routine is thrown off."

Mark raised an eyebrow in challenge. Xavier had never been a routine kind of person. He thrived as a creative soul, following the music as it flowed from one melody to the next—not that there had been any music lately.

"I'm working on it." Xavier headed to the kitchen, wondering if that sour smell in the air had been here when they left this morning. Working quickly, he tied off the garbage bag and lifted it from the container. "Cody, come take this out, please."

Cody set aside the phone with a sigh. "Sure, Dad." He plodded over and took the bag.

"Are you going to say hi to our guest?" Xavier prodded.

Cody nodded as if he'd resigned himself to a task. "Hey, Uncle Mark."

They bumped fists.

Xavier twisted his lips as he thought about what just happened. Did Cody not feel like an important part of things around here? They were home all day together, but he wasn't sure how much they talked. Was his son lonely? Or was he lacking in energy because of the diabetes? If that was the case, what was Xavier supposed to do about it? There were pamphlets in the car and an internet full of advice—he needed to roll up his sleeves and start educating himself. But that wasn't going to take care of the mess. "Maybe we need to hire a maid."

Mark frowned. "You need a cleaning crew, a life coach, and a chef."

"Like I can afford all that."

"Or …" Mark checked the counter for anything sticky before leaning against it and folding his arms. "Hear me out on this one. There is another option."

"Yeah?" Xavier opened the dishwasher to find it empty. Great. He could load it all that much faster. "Like what?"

"You could get remarried."

Xavier dropped the plastic plate on the floor. He glared at Mark. "That's not funny."

Mark rubbed the back of his neck. "I wasn't joking. This is not living! You're barely functioning. It kills me to see a man with your talent wasting away, and Cody deserves to know how amazing his father actually is. But you're lost. Are you still grieving Nora?"

Xavier swooped down and retrieved the plate. "No. I miss her, but the pain and the sorrow aren't there like they were. I just … I just don't know how to make each day special like she did."

Mark smiled. "Women have that gift. They can turn an ordinary afternoon into the best day of your life."

Xavier nodded. "Truth." A few years ago, he might have turned that phrase into a hit country song.

"Look, I'm not saying you should, or even could, replace Nora. But you need to think about getting married again. You wrote your best stuff when you had a partner."

Xavier's mouth went dry. "It's not that easy."

"Don't overthink it."

Xavier put in the last glass and added soap. "Why are you harping on this? What's your angle?"

Mark grinned like the Big Bad Wolf. "I have a meeting with Tyson Temple in six weeks. He wants something different—something fresh. I think he'd love your music. But I haven't got anything to offer him."

Tyson was the owner of one of the biggest labels in country music. He wore a ten-gallon hat and alligator boots with an attitude. If a songwriter got in with him, he was in for life. Rumor was he'd built a mansion in Moose Creek, but if he lived here, he kept to himself. "Pull out the old stuff." Xavier tucked his head and grabbed a washcloth. He doused it in the sink and scrubbed at the mound of old ketchup dried on the counter.

"He's heard it. He likes your sound, but he wants new material."

Curses. "I haven't got anything new." He scrubbed harder at the stain.

Mark squared his shoulders. "Xavier, I'm not going to lie to you— this is a make-or-break-your-career moment. You need to pull your act together and give me a song that I can present to this guy."

Make or break—words he'd hoped he'd never hear but had known were coming. He'd stockpiled songs—they'd poured out of him while Nora was pregnant—and not thought a thing of it, writing for six to eight hours a day while she was at work, and then they'd spend their evenings dreaming about this beautiful little life they'd created. That stockpile had kept the money coming in for several years after her death. But the checks were smaller and smaller each month, and his stockpile was now an empty folder. He didn't have other skills. Sure, he could find work, but not the kind that fed his soul.

He stared down at the cloth. "And you think getting a wife will help me write again?"

"You've never done well in chaos. Look around you, man. A wife brings order, health, comfort, and joy—all the things you're missing."

The whole idea was preposterous—too big to take on in one bite. "Where am I even supposed to find a wife?"

"Go online. E-date."

"Sounds … impersonal." And kind of perfect, actually. He didn't want a wife to warm his bed. That level of closeness was scary. Loving a person meant being vulnerable to the pain of losing them. He'd already been through that and couldn't imagine doing it again. But if he could find someone who could help him be a better father and with Cody's prediabetes, well, that was reason enough to tie the knot. He'd do anything for his son. And with Cody squared away, he might be able to visit with his muse. What they were doing now wasn't working. He'd have to change if he wanted a different outcome than the one he faced every morning.

Mark continued, "It's how dating works these days. You've been out of the game for a while."

"I guess so." Xavier picked up a pile of unopened mail and moved it to the table so he could wipe underneath it. He'd have to go through that pile … sometime. Probably not today. There were so many other things he should work on. He just didn't know where to start, and so he probably wouldn't. "I'll get working on a song." He glanced at the door to his music room. It had been shut for so long he'd have to excavate his keyboard from the dust.

Cody came back inside, his face red and sweat beading at his hairline from his efforts and the summer temps. He went for the fridge and pulled out a soda, taking a long plug.

Xavier hesitated, taking the soda from him. "Do you want some water?" he asked.

"I'm good. Thanks, though." Cody headed back to the couch, where he settled in to finish his movie. Xavier would let him finish off the sodas in the fridge and then not buy more. They'd both be forced to drink water for a while. It would be better for both of them.

Mark checked his watch. "I've got to get going. I'll text you the date Tyson is coming to be in town."

"Sounds great. I'll be ready." Even as he said the words, he wondered if they were true. He had no ideas, no inspiration, no hope of coming up with a new song in six weeks. Mark would be forced to drop him as a client, and he'd be officially washed up.

What a depressing thought.

Mark said goodbye to Cody and then went out the front door.

Xavier ignored the mess in the front room and headed to his bedroom. His laptop was on the nightstand. He propped himself up with pillows and began scanning websites on childhood diabetes. The information wasn't encouraging and was most definitely overwhelming. He zoned out after the third link, afraid of what would happen to his son—what his life would be like. Needles. Insulin. One page mentioned the problems teens had feeling like they fit in while knowing they were different from their peers. He stared off to the side of the screen. He needed help. Thinking about Mark's advice to find a wife, he browsed an online dating site.

The smiling faces and bright colors seemed so ... optimistic. These ladies were looking for the love of their life. They didn't want what he had to offer—which wasn't much, once he thought about it. He was asking a woman to move in, become a mother, keep house, cook, and be his partner in a songwriting business. What would she get in return? Well ... room and board. And Cody was in school, so she'd have hours to dedicate to her own interests. He could also be her friend. Her best friend, if she wanted. And he was loyal. Not every man could boast that quality.

He didn't need to e-date. He needed a hiring service. But it wasn't like there were employment agencies for brides.

Okay. So. His next option was to write an ad. Like in the *Moose Creek Matchmaker*. Locals were constantly putting in ads for everything from aboveground swimming pools to ski gear and jobs from master carpenter to laundress. If you had something to barter or sell or needed to purchase an odd item, then the *Matchmaker* was your source.

He logged onto their website and filled out the first part of the advertising form with his name and credit card info. He checked the box that kept his identity a secret. The site would collect responses instead of sending them to his email account and giving away his name. He wasn't hugely famous, but a Google search would tell people what he did for a living and who he'd sold songs to in the past. He had some pretty big hits—and the awards to prove it. He didn't want a woman who was interested in starting her own writing career and using him as a stepping stone.

The ad would run him ten dollars a day. He opted for one day to test the waters. If nothing came of it, then he'd look into other options. He really, really didn't want to ask his parents to set him up. They wouldn't understand why he'd want to be married to someone he wasn't in love with. He'd had love—that kind of connection with a person didn't happen twice in a lifetime.

He stared at the box where he was supposed to type his ad.

Wanted: A wife.

He took a deep breath in and blew it out slowly, his lips forming an O. Typing that felt big. So big.

Cody appeared in his doorway. "I don't feel good. I'm going back to bed."

The doctor said that fatigue was one of the symptoms, and the soda had probably upset his stomach. "Okay, bud. I'll come check on you in a minute."

"'Kay." He plodded off.

Xavier stared after him. Really, it didn't matter if this woman could help him write or not. What was most important was Cody's health. He needed someone who could save his son. He typed faster, afraid he'd lose his nerve if he didn't get this done.

Requirements:

1. *Over 26*
2. *Cooks healthy meals*
3. *Active lifestyle*

4. *Loves children (I have 1)*

LOOKING *for a best friend to partner with for life.*
   No intimacy required.

HE GAGGED at the last line, but how else was he going to get across the fact that he wanted a platonic relationship? Still, he was a writer by trade; he should have done better. Before his internal editor could take over, he hit send.

"That was either brilliant or stupid," he said to the empty room.

He'd know by noon tomorrow which one it was.

2

EMILY

*E*mily Wilson blinked and pushed the *Matchmaker* away from her face so her eyes could focus on the strange ad. "Wanted: a Wife." She blinked again. It really said that. The *Matchmaker* was a local paper that had a few articles but mostly classifieds for garage and estate sales and appliances. Occasionally, someone would put in a job offer or was looking for a specific skill, like welding or refurbishing a violin.

She skimmed the rest of the ad, worried because a part of her whispered *apply*. She'd just turned 29, hadn't dated anyone seriously in four years, and wanted to be a mom.

But there was no way becoming a mother and having a family could be that easy ... could it?

"Are we going to start soon?" asked Mrs. Maxwell. She wore leopard-print yoga pants with a black top today. Her husband was a bigwig in the entertainment industry, and Mrs. Maxwell always dressed like she'd walked off the pages of a fashion magazine.

"You bet." Emily glanced around the room, noting that all the regulars were in place with their yoga mats rolled out in front of them and their shoes lined up next to the mats.

A gentleman with gray temples and a nice build entered. "Am I in the right place?"

Emily smiled. Her room was just off the regular workout space with weights and machines. "Yoga?"

"Whatever gets me ready for ski season." He went to the back of the room, grabbed a mat, and rolled it out without saying another word.

Oh-kay. She dropped the *Matchmaker* onto her desk and hurried to take her place. "How are we feeling today? Is anyone in pain?"

No one raised their hand. The beautiful thing about teaching a yoga class for people who had arthritis was that she could modify the class for a particular person's comfort if needed. In the winter, they adjusted often, but since summer was in full swing, they were able to jump right in.

The yoga class was the one part of her job as a physical therapist she looked forward to. Pushing patients to the limits of pain and physical abilities didn't bring her the satisfaction she'd seen in her coworkers. She liked helping people and was active, so PT seemed like a good idea.

She'd known there would be hours indoors, but she didn't know how much it would wear on her. Her dad called her a "drop of sunshine," but she'd come to learn that she had to recharge in the sun often to keep that happy spark alive.

She took the class through several poses, her thoughts drawn back to that strange ad. She pictured several different kinds of men posting it. Desperate men. Scoundrels misrepresenting themselves. But the idea that came back over and over again was of a guy who was lonely and tired of dating games. She was pretty tired of them herself.

As she walked through the room to check her students' form, she noticed the new guy grimacing. She grabbed a block and placed it on the floor next to his hand. "If you use this, you'll keep your balance and won't strain."

He stared at her chest, which was right at eye level as he bent over. "That's some good customer service."

She grimaced, searching for a way out of the situation that didn't involve telling him to move his eyes up, which would embarrass her and the rest of her students. She remembered what he'd said about skiing. "We're all about getting stronger in here, so you don't get hurt on the slopes."

"It's nice to know you're watching out for me." His tone was flirty. "I'm from out of town, and you're making me feel very welcome."

The way he talked made it sound like she was encouraging him in a way she hadn't intended to. Feeling like there was a worm on her neck she wanted to swat away, she smiled woodenly and moved on to help the next person.

When class was over, Mrs. Maxwell stopped to pat her arm. "You're such a darling." She wiped her damp hair out of her face. "Thank you for class." Mrs. Maxwell's arthritis had come on a few years ago. She'd been able to get it into remission last year. Emily hoped it stayed that way.

"You're so welcome." Emily tightened her ponytail, which had come lose during a downward-facing dog. "You did great today. You're really sinking into those poses with confidence."

"I feel more confident. Thanks." She winked and trailed out behind the other class members.

Emily wandered to her desk, her mind back on that ad. What a strange thing to think about—*applying* to be a man's wife.

Even so, part of Emily wondered what made a man so open. It took guts to post an ad like that. Had he suffered a broken heart? Was his child in need of a mother? Her own mother was the heart and hearth of their home. Her heart went out to this stranger.

She marked down the number of students she'd had today. With that done, she could meet Mr. Maxwell to work on his bum knee. There might just be tears today, and she wasn't looking forward to the session. Gearing herself up, she wasn't looking where she was going and

ran into the hard chest of the new guy. "Oh, excuse me. I didn't see you there." She laughed lightly, waiting for him to back up.

He didn't. "Would you like to go to dinner with me tonight?"

She chewed her lip. He wasn't really her type. His hair was combed slick and straight, like an older version of James Bond. And his eyes were steel gray, a shade that sent shivers down her back—and not the good kind. "I already have plans." She purposefully kept it vague. He didn't need to know that her plans included ice cream and Netflix.

He stepped closer. She stepped back, keeping her personal space the same. He moved forward again, and her back was against the wall. On her right was the desk. She could climb over it. As if reading her mind, his hand landed next to her shoulder on the brick, blocking her in.

"I was promised a good time this week," he said low and husky, his eyes dipping to places they shouldn't have.

"Not by me!" She shoved against him, noting the harsh smell of his aftershave.

He leaned into her, pinning her with his chest. Her heartbeat and her vocal cords locked in place. She couldn't fight. She couldn't run. She was frozen with fear that spiked through her and locked her limbs in place.

"I'll forgive you." He kissed her bare shoulder.

"Stop." She squeezed the word out, mortified that she could barely hear it.

He chuckled cruelly, and his lips vibrated against her skin as he worked his way along her collarbone. "I was going to buy you dinner first. But I don't mind skipping the meal."

"No." She willed her hands to shove against him, to resist, but they were clamped in place. He grabbed at her body, roaming his hands over the back side of her yoga pants.

There were people close. They would help her. They just needed to hear. She drew in a shaky breath, swallowed, and yelled, "Help!"

His beefy hand clamped over her mouth.

"Hey!" barked Dan, one of the other PTs.

Her attacker backed away. "Sorry." He faked chagrin. "We should keep it professional in the office, babe."

Her hands and legs shook. She stayed against the wall, needing help to stand.

Dan watched the guy saunter out before noticing her state. "Em, you okay?"

She fell forward, holding her arms across her middle. "He attacked me." She wretched out the words. "He sat in my class and then he, he …"

Dan helped her into a chair. He pulled out his phone and dialed. "I'd like to report an assault." His voice moved to the background as she rocked, too stunned to cry.

Her eyes landed on the ad in the paper. Her world suddenly didn't make sense. She wasn't safe here. She didn't even like it here. Yet she'd stayed because her education had cost a pretty penny and she'd felt obligated to follow through.

Something inside of her whispered that she should make a change —a big one. Get out of the gym. Find a new life where she enjoyed getting up each morning. One where she could be safe.

She picked up a pen and drew a slow, perfect circle around the ad.

TWO DAYS LATER, Emily went back to the office to pick up her last paycheck. She'd taken a job she didn't love and therefore didn't care enough to go back after the assault, other than making sure she was paid what she was due. The scales had fallen away from her consciousness, and she'd decided to find her passion.

When she looked back on the assault, she decided it could have been much worse. She could also see that it *was* horrible. No one should have to go through what she did, and she was proud of herself for pressing charges right away.

The police had arrested the man—Roger. He'd spent a night in custody before his girlfriend posted bail. His *girlfriend!* Emily wanted to tell her to run away. Run far, far away from the monster.

She kept her chin up as she went through the automatic doors. Charity, another PT, ran across the room and threw her arms around

Emily's neck, holding so tight Emily gasped for air when she finally let go.

"How are you doing?" Charity asked, her eyes full of sympathy and ... something more, a knowledge of the shock and sense of having your safety stripped away. Charity understood—maybe she'd even been there before.

Emily wasn't about to ask her, but she placed her hand on top of Charity's and looked right in her eyes, letting her know that she understood too. "I'm doing okay."

"Good." Charity squeezed her arms again. "I'm going to miss you." She hugged her once more and then turned to walk with her to the HR desk, where her check waited. It was nice to have someone to walk with her, someone close. There were people all around, and that helped too. She'd thought she'd be overcome with memories or flashbacks, but that didn't happen. She wasn't going to walk into her old room and tempt fate.

Emily had a short convo with Karyn about wrapping up her employment. As she was standing there, her eyes caught on the *Matchmaker* with a perfect circle drawn around an ad. The circle triggered a memory, something about sitting at the desk after the attack. She couldn't grab onto it with both mental hands, but her curiosity was piqued. The paper was printed three times a week; this couldn't be the same one that had been on her desk the day she was attacked.

"Can I see that?" She pointed to the paper.

Karyn glanced down. "Oh, yeah." She stopped typing and handed her the page. "That ads created quite a stir around town. Everyone is talking about it."

"Really?" Emily hadn't been out much, holing up with her sister and watching chick flicks that reminded her there were good men in the world. "What's the buzz?" Dang, it felt good to talk about something other than herself and her feelings—to just feel normal for a minute. She scanned the ad again.

"Well, my sister thinks the guy is a nutjob, but my sister-in-law thinks he's lonely and desperate."

Emily smiled. "What do you think?"

"I think it's kind of sad. To advertise for a companion like that—how lonely does a person have to be?" She went back to clicking and clacking.

I fit the description. Healthy. Cooks. I'm 29 and a half. Emily's heart began to burn inside of her, urging her to send in a reply. "What do they think of the women who answered him?" she mumbled.

"Oh goodness, no one's crazy enough to respond to that rubbish." Karyn snatched several sheets out of the warm printer and handed them over. "Here's the letter of recommendation Mr. Samson promised you, and your check. You're all set." Her shoulders and the corners of her mouth lowered. "I'm sad to see you go."

The kind words were another balm to Emily's wounds. She may not have loved working here, but she did like the people she worked with—they were positive, helpful, generous, and generally watched out for one another. "I am too." Right at that moment, she was disheartened to think she wouldn't be coming in here every day. She left, waving at the regulars and her ex-coworkers on the way out.

Once she was outside the glass double doors, all she had to do was turn her face to the sunshine to know she'd made the right decision.

Something crinkled under her arm, and she looked down to find the *Matchmaker* tucked there. Not knowing when she had taken it with her, she held it out in front of her. A sense of calm and purpose filled her heart. She typed out a quick response to the ad on her phone, including that she wasn't looking for romance or sex, but a friend would be nice. As a final touch, she snapped a picture of her letter of recommendation and sent the whole thing off to the email address indicated before she changed her mind.

Her phone rang, and she answered for her sister. Poor Lexi was probably wondering if Emily would have rent money this month. Her sister sank everything she had into the condo they shared, going on faith that the Lord would help her make the payments. "Hey," Emily said by way of greeting.

"Hey yourself. I don't suppose you changed your mind on quitting."

Emily stretched her free arm out, letting the mountain heat roast against her skin. "Nope."

"Well, then I guess it's a good thing I just found us a roommate."

"Really?" Lexi had been advertising the third bedroom for months. "That's great. Especially considering the fact that I may be moving out."

"What?!" Her shriek was loud enough that several heads turned Emily's way as she headed to her car in the parking lot.

"I, uh, applied for a new position, and it comes with room and board."

"Where?" Lexi demanded.

Emily chewed her thumbnail, suddenly nervous about her decision that only moments before had felt so right. "Remember the ad for a wife?"

"You didn't."

"I did."

"Are you crazy?"

"I prefer the term *inspired*."

"What are you going to do if he contacts you?"

"I'll go for an interview." She unlocked her car and climbed in. The heat grabbed onto her and warmed her all the way to her bones. She smiled even as she slammed the key in the ignition so she could roll down the windows.

"You don't interview a husband—you date him."

"I think he'll be interviewing me. And isn't it the same thing?"

"No, it's not the same. And that's even more of a reason to withdraw your application."

Emily sighed. "There is one thing that worries me." She glanced in the rearview mirror at her thick eyelashes, which looked stunning with several coats of coal-black mascara. She loved the new swoop she'd started doing with her liner; it opened up her blue eyes and made them pop.

"*One* thing?"

"I get the feeling that he's looking for someone a little more *motherly*." She wasn't the type to wear mom jeans. She liked yoga pants and wearing Barbie ponytails. If she showed up looking like a girl who lived at the gym, he might think she wasn't the type for the job. But she also really loved wearing makeup, having shiny hair, and looking like a woman.

"Why do you think that?"

"The ad mentioned his child and he wanted someone over 26, so I think he's looking for a certain maturity level."

Lexi laughed. "And how are you going to look like a mom?"

Emily made a face. "I'll figure it out."

"Good luck with that."

"Your sarcasm is not welcome here." The air conditioner kicked on and blew lukewarm air into the vehicle. Emily welcomed it, checked her mirrors, and backed out.

Lexi huffed. "Well, maybe my advice will be welcome. Do *not* marry a stranger. It's insane." She paused. "Are you in some kind of shock because of the assault? What does your counselor say?"

The police had given Emily the number for a local counselor. She'd seen her twice in the last 48 hours. While she might always have some triggers, she'd been reassured that overall, she was mentally stable and able to function well in society.

"Actually, I was thinking of applying before the attack even happened. So there." Her phone dinged. Stopping at the entrance to the lot, she glanced at her phone. "Umm …"

"What?" Lexi asked in that tone that she'd used when they were kids and Emily had to stop to tie her shoes *again*.

"He answered me back." Emily grinned as she read through the invitation to meet at a coffee shop the next day. "I have to go." She needed to hit the thrift store and find something to wear.

"See? He's already separating you from the people who love you."

She laughed, feeling like she was on the right track for the first time in a long time. Long before the assault, even before moving back to Moose Creek. "I'll let you know if he turns out to be a serial killer."

"How will you let me know? You'll be dead."

"I'll haunt you," Emily joked.

"You'd better," Lexi replied, letting her know that she wasn't too serious about

Emily said goodbye and hung up. She took a good look in the mirror, wondering if she was actually crazy. Then, she decided that crazy people don't ask that question, so she must be sane. With a wink at herself, she took the next opening into traffic.

3

XAVIER

A light breeze tugged at napkins and lifted the American flag hanging on the back of the small mountainside café. Xavier sat on the deck, watching a family from Texas paddleboard around the small lake. Their accents were heavy and their children respectful even as they splashed each other. They all wore Texas University ball hats, cutoff jeans, and smiles. The attendant who rented out the paddleboards sat on a three-legged stool and read a novel.

Xavier glanced covertly at the other people at the coffee shop enjoying the morning temperatures. He'd started quite the buzz around Moose Creek with his ad. Everywhere he went, people talked about it.

The cashier at the grocery store had gossiped as she scanned his TV dinners and frozen pizzas. "I'll bet he's 73 and has hair growing out of his ears." She'd nodded deeply. "No man with half good looks would need to beg for a wife."

Xavier had bristled. "Maybe he's not looking for that kind of a wife. It said he wanted a friend."

"Lies—men will say anything to get a woman these days. Why, I was online just the other night …"

He'd tuned out her horror story of online dating and began

bagging his groceries himself, making as much noise as possible shaking each bag open and rustling his hand inside. By then, the woman behind him in line had picked up the conversation. His ears burned as he hurried out the sliding doors and he'd decided to give up the search.

And then he'd gotten *her* email.

Emily.

Her answer was sweet and to the point, and it spoke to his soul. That was the songwriter inside of him coming out, but it was true. Even her name was like a cupcake with beautifully swirled frosting and sprinkles on top.

He'd gotten some weird responses to the ad. One woman wanted him to fingerprint himself and send her the prints so she could forward them on to her cousin at the FBI, who would do a full background check. Yeah, because that was going to happen.

One woman asked to bring her four cats, one of which was expecting a litter any day now. Sorry. No.

Another wanted their union blessed by a rabbi, a priest, and an internet clergyman. At that point, he'd decided his life had become the punch line of a bad joke.

And then there was Emily. No love. No romance. And a letter of recommendation from a reputable source. She was perfect on paper. He planned to offer her the position—as long as she was more friend than friendly during this meeting. If she came on to him at all, he'd have to give up this crazy idea and at least hire a cook.

He tugged at his shirt collar. Even worse than her flirting would be if *he* was attracted to *her*. Distractions were his downfall when it came to writing songs. A beautiful woman traipsing about his house would surely pull his head out of the creative process and turn it towards less productive thoughts.

"Xavier?" asked a woman in cargo shorts to her knees and a loose Elvis Presley T-shirt. "I'm Emily."

He stood out of respect and shook her outstretched hand. She had her hair pulled back in a messy bun and a blue bandanna tied with the knot on the top of her head. Her face was free of makeup, and she wore hiking shoes with low socks. Her whole look screamed *I love the outdoors*.

He breathed a sigh of relief that Emily wasn't his type. Nora had been refined, wearing slacks and blouses, pearls and diamonds on a daily basis. Her black hair had been cut in a straight line, and she'd studied the violin. Emily's nails were short and her nose slightly sunburnt. "It's nice to meet you."

"You too." She pulled out her own chair and sat down. He stood for a minute, feeling lost without having been a gentleman, before taking his seat.

"What made you—?" They both started and cut off.

"You first." He held a hand out for her to start.

She glanced around the deck to make sure they weren't overheard. Her cautiousness made him feel more secure with her. He'd been worried about meeting up with her in public, afraid she'd alert the local new station and they'd show up with cameras and questions. His stomach stopped rolling.

"What made you place the ad?" she asked.

He debated how much to tell her. He could go all the way back to his and Nora's wedding, to Nora's death during childbirth, or start with Cody's diagnosis.

He must have hesitated too long, because she leaned forward. "Maybe I should tell you why I'm here."

The tension in his forehead released, and he leaned forward on the table, mirroring her posture. "Do tell."

She smiled slightly, but her eyes didn't light up. For some reason, that bothered him. His first impression of her was that she was someone who had a lot of spirit and commanded a room. He got the feeling that her inner light was muted—perhaps by a broken heart or maybe a trauma in her past. His interest in her grew and he inched closer, wondering if he could coax that light to shine.

"I've always wanted to be a mom. I have the best parents in the whole world—seriously. They made being parents look like fun. I know it's not all roses and rainbows, but I feel like I'd be good at parenting. The, uh, opportunity hasn't come up for me. Now ..." She held up a palm. "I understand that I won't actually be your child's parent. I just—I have all these mothering instincts yearning to come out of me."

"Like what?" Cody didn't need a woman moving in who was going to smother him, no matter how good her intentions. His son was … well, he wasn't sure how to describe him. They lived together, and yet they were independent men.

"Like reading bedtime stories and baking cookies, taking first-day-of-school pictures and creating science projects—all of it." She clasped her hands together and then laid them flat on the table.

"That doesn't sound so bad."

She laughed, and the world suddenly got brighter. "I should hope not."

He stared at her, wondering if he'd imagined the difference in a world where her laughter tickled the air. After a moment, he took off his sunglasses and cleaned them on the hem of his shirt. He wasn't used to being around women who were as real as Emily. That must have been the reason that his world seemed to stop the moment she smiled.

She glanced down at her hands, biting her bottom lip. It took him a moment more to realize that his silence was causing her discomfort.

"Sorry. I—" There were no good words to use an excuse, so he jumped into his reasoning for placing the ad. He explained about the prediabetes and his creative soul that didn't allow him to create order but thrived inside of it nonetheless.

She nodded along. "So basically, I'll be getting two children to care for."

A laugh burst from him, so startling that *he* jumped. Then he laughed at himself right along with her. "I think that about covers it."

She shrugged. "I can live with that. I'll need time to myself, time to see my family, some vacation time—I like to hike, and Peru has been calling my name."

He liked that she knew these things about herself and that she was confident to ask for them up front. No games. No mind reading. No guessing. He'd had to do a lot of that with Nora. Admittedly, he wasn't very good at it. Writing her a song usually got him out of the doghouse. "That sounds good. We can write up a contract just between us."

"Whatever you're comfortable with. But I have to ask, why marriage? Why not just hire a nanny?"

His cheeks flushed with heat. "I'm old-fashioned. I don't want to live with a woman unless I'm married to her."

Emily's lips formed a perfect O. He'd never seen lips so ... round. "Well, I can respect that, and thanks for respecting me."

He nodded. "My mama raised me right."

"I certainly hope so." She cocked her head. "You know people are talking about that ad—my sister's worried you're a serial killer."

"I promise you, I'm not."

"That's exactly what a serial killer would say." Her eyes fairly danced with mirth.

He feigned nonchalance. "The only way to prove it is to not kill you in the woods."

"I'd appreciate that."

"Consider it done." He held out his hand. "Will you marry me?"

She laughed. "I think this is the beginning of a beautiful friendship."

She slipped her hand into his. His skin tingled as if charged with static electricity. Once they shook, he rubbed his palm on his leg to get rid of the feeling.

They made plans to meet at the courthouse on Thursday. She had a few things to wrap up before she got married, and he needed to explain to Cody that their lives were about to change—hopefully for the better. He stared at his hand, where the tingling lingered. Yes, Emily was going to make changes. He only hoped they were both ready for them.

4

EMILY

*T*he thrift store smelled like mothballs. Emily wrinkled her nose as the scent attacked her from all sides.

Lexi rolled her eyes. "When you said 'shopping for your new job,' I thought we'd be at the Nike outlet." They crossed the chipped cream tile to the women's section and began sifting through the mounds of clothing.

Lexi held up a pair of raspberry sweatpants with a tapered ankle. "Is this what you're looking for?"

Emily squinted as she considered them. They were bagging in all the right places. "Yep. Thanks."

"You could have saved yourself four dollars and borrowed them from Grandma."

"Har har har." Emily tucked her hair behind her ear and kept looking. She grabbed a pair of mom jeans one size too big and tossed them over her elbow. "You don't get it. When we shook hands, there was this zing up my arm. He totally felt it too, and then he acted like I'd infected him with something and wiped his hand on his pants. He doesn't want feminine wiles. I have to look as grungy as possible."

"So your regular yoga pants and running tops?"

"Out. I'll bury them in the back of my closet."

They dug for a few more minutes. Lexi came up with a light-blue shirt with three kittens on the front.

"You have amazing taste." Emily snatched the shirt away.

"It's a gift." She blew on her fingernails and buffed them against her shoulder. "So what's this guy's deal?"

The question had been long coming, but Emily had been able to sidestep it so far. The things Xavier shared were … personal. He spoke low, as if he wasn't used to confiding in anyone. What a sad, lonely life. Her heart ached for him. And yet, he didn't seem aware enough of his own feelings of loss to process them despite the evidence painted in his eyes. She went for the edited version. "He's widowed. You should have heard him talk about his dead wife. He only said, like, seven words, but there was this reverence for her. I'm glad I'm not trying to win his heart, because it's firmly in her hands. He really does just want a friend and co-parent. He's really quite … sweet."

"Sweet like an ax murderer," Lexi mumbled.

Emily stifled her grin. She'd enjoyed joking with Xavier about that —it was morbid and weird but right up her alley with sarcasm. "He has a great sense of humor. I can see myself getting along with him for the rest of our lives."

"And you know this after one meeting?"

She thought back to the comfort and peace that accompanied their time together, the way conversation flowed, and how they were able to make plans for the wedding by resolving scheduling conflicts without conflict. "Yeah. Sometimes you just know." She headed to the changing rooms.

"Fine. But what are you going to tell Mom and Dad?"

Emily stopped mid-step. "I'm not. And neither are you."

"You can't *not* tell them you got married." Lexi grabbed her by the shoulders and gave her a shake.

"I can … *not*. I mean, it's fine. I want to see if it takes first. You know how they are about marriage. They'd totally freak out if they knew I wasn't marrying Xavier for love."

"I'm still not sure why you're marrying him at all."

Emily bit back her answer. Being a mom was the biggest wish of her heart, and while she'd felt safe sharing it with Xavier because she felt like he'd understand, Lexi might not. After all, women weren't encouraged to be moms these days. They were supposed to go after a career and find fulfillment. But there was a part of her that wouldn't ever be filled unless she became a mother. "It's just something I have to do," she almost whispered.

Lexi hooked her arm around Emily's neck and gave her a tight hug. "Then I'm all in with you."

"You're the best sister ever."

"I know."

They laughed together. As Emily tried on the mom jeans and kitten shirt, she couldn't help but wonder how getting married was going to change her relationship with her sister. Marriage, as her parents had shown, was supposed to be the most important relationship in your life. She willed her hands to stop shaking, even as she prayed she was up to the task ahead.

5

XAVIER

"So she's going to move in with us. Are you okay with that?" Xavier kicked himself for not talking to Cody before he'd placed the ad. This was as much his decision as it was Xavier's. Okay, maybe not *as much,* but he should have had a say in things.

If Cody was upset, he'd call off the wedding. There was no way he could traumatize his child on purpose. Being a parent was hard enough when he was trying to do the right thing. Purposely putting Cody in a situation that he'd need therapy for later in life was not going to win him any parenting awards.

The thought of telling Emily this wasn't going to work made his heart sink. She'd been so happy talking about things like science projects and bedtime stories. He wanted to make her happy. On top of that, Emily was the answer to his prayers. He knew it and he knew God knew it, and if he backed out, there'd be a day of reckoning.

"Is she in charge of me?" Cody asked.

Xavier debated how to answer that. "Yes. Like when you go to school and your teacher is in charge. That's how Emily will be here."

Cody plucked at the loose fabric on the couch, making Xavier wonder how long ago he'd bought the furniture. He glanced around, noting the shabby appearance to things that had once been a source of pride. Losing his wife had taken many things from him, but he hadn't even noticed his dignity—or maybe it was arrogance—slipping away. The first song he sold, he would buy new living room furniture. Emily could pick it out. Wait—maybe not. Considering her outdoorsy appearance, she'd probably pick something camouflage. While it would certainly be rugged and definitely manly, he wasn't sure he'd enjoy that décor. They'd go shopping together.

"Okay." Cody hopped off the couch. "Can I play now?" His hands were already reaching for the controller on the coffee table.

The doorbell rang. "That's Mark. You can have twenty minutes, and then you need to read for a while."

"'Kay." Cody clicked several buttons, and the television came to life.

Mark let himself in with a "Hello!"

"In here." Xavier made his way to the kitchen, where he pulled a frozen pizza out and ripped open the box.

Mark ambled in just as he set the timer on the stove. "Cardboard for dinner—yum." He loosened his tie. Dressed in his agent attire, he threw a leg over a barstool and took a seat.

"Don't knock it till you try it." Xavier shut the oven door and brushed off his hands. "I have good news."

Mark perked up. "You finished a song?"

"No. But I found a wife."

His mouth fell open. "You did what now?"

"I placed an ad in the paper, and I found a wife. We're getting married tomorrow."

"You're joking."

"No."

Mark slapped a hand to his forehead. "You're insane." He jumped off the stool and paced in front of the island. "You're the guy everyone is talking about. Do you know what they're saying?"

Xavier frowned. "Some of it. It's not flattering."

"Because you don't advertise for a bride! You go online and advertise yourself—hoping the right woman will come along and actually see your profile picture."

Xavier wrinkled his nose. "Sounds like fishing."

"This isn't funny. Your reputation is hanging by a thread as it is. If word gets out that you're the newspaper ad guy, then you'll never sell another song again."

"First of all, that mode of dating doesn't make any sense. It's not about who was looking for me; it's about who I was looking for." He snapped his fingers. "You should start a new dating site. People can place ads like the one I put out, and women and men can apply. You'd make a killing!

"Secondly, Emily is as normal as they come. There's nothing crazy or weird about her. She is interesting and down-to-earth."

Mark folded his arms. "If she's normal, then why is she marrying you?"

"Funny." He smirked.

Mark leaned forward and pressed the tips of his fingers together. "I'm not joking. What's wrong with a woman that she'd answer an ad like that?"

"Nothing! She wants to be a mom." He glanced around Mark to make sure Cody wasn't listening. "And from what I saw on her letter of recommendation, she's exactly what Cody needs. She's a physical therapist with a fitness degree and comes from a solid family. She's into the outdoors. I want to take her and Cody to the cabin for a couple weeks. They can explore while I write. I don't think Cody has every really gone outside while we're up there."

"You're going to let her alone with your child?"

"People do it all the time with daycare, and there's no guarantee those people are normal."

"There's a little one—they have to be certified by the state."

"They do?" Xavier didn't know that. The timer dinged, and he used a giant spatula to scoop the pizza off the oven rack and set it on the granite counter to cool. "I didn't know that."

Mark pinched the bridge of his nose. "You can back out."

Xavier busied himself looking for the pizza cutter. He finally found it in the dishwasher with the clean dishes. He mulled over the idea of turning Emily away, and a sense of darkness overcame him. "I don't want to." The words gave him a sliver of light, and he grabbed on to it, realizing as he did that he was holding the memory of her laughter mingling with his. Somehow, in the forty minutes they'd spent talking, she'd brightened his world and gotten him to laugh from his belly. His stomach muscles were still complaining about it. They hadn't been used in years—not to laugh, anyway. The slight tightness told him that his life had been grays and browns for too long. "I'm going to marry her," he stated with firmness. "I feel like this is the right thing to do, and I know she can help Cody. I'd do anything to save him."

Mark dropped his arms to his sides in defeat and then bolstered himself. "I hope it works out for you." He took the first slice of pizza and blew on the cheese before tasting it. He bobbed his head in approval. "And if it does work out for you, maybe I'll place an ad for a bride."

"Let me write it for you," Xavier teased. "No woman wants your legalese proposal."

Mark looked around for a napkin. "You mock me now. My ad would bring in the ladies."

Xavier snorted. "Whatever." *I already got the best of the bunch.* He hid his smile behind a piece of steaming hot pizza.

"I still think you're nuts. And when this whole thing goes south, I know a guy who can get you a quick annulment. Hey, maybe you'll get some breakup songs out of it." He finished off his slice and wiped his fingers clean.

Xavier's heart sank. He didn't want this marriage to fail. He wanted to make a friend who would be a co-parent he could count on. What had his dad told him on his wedding day—his *first* wedding day? "Be the type of person you would want to be married to." He vowed right then and there to do his best to be a partner. He could do that. He *would* do that. Then Emily would have no reason to leave.

A whisper of fear ran through him. What if she didn't show up to the wedding? Or worse, what if she was here for weeks or months and decided he was too high-maintenance for her? He shoved the storm clouds away. Emily wasn't going to leave. She was committed to their future marriage.

Over the course of the evening, fear would creep in and he'd repeat his earlier words. Emily wasn't going to leave him. He knew the fear came from Nora's death. She hadn't volunteered to make him a single parent, but she had nonetheless. Emily was different. She was healthy —robust, even—where Nora had been frail. Emily wasn't going to die. They were going to be together for a long time—maybe even after Cody was grown up. He'd be happy to live with his best friend forever.

6

EMILY

*E*mily glanced down at the pathetic flats on her feet. They had a scuff on the outside of the right shoe. Her flour sack of a dress hung on her frame, and she'd worn her hair in a messy bun at the base of her neck. Not exactly the blushing bride, she nevertheless flushed with heat when the justice of the peace told Xavier to kiss his wife.

Her heart thundered inside her chest as she slowly lifted her gaze to meet his. Two blue pools of panic might as well have been a mirror into her soul. She lifted her fist up.

He caught on quick and brushed his knuckles against hers.

The whole thing was ridiculous and stupid and made her giggle. They were crazy for getting married, and the sensations made her punch drunk. His shoulders began to shake with barely controlled laughter. By the time the ceremony concluded, they were both holding their bellies and laughing too loud to hear the pronouncement.

She swiped the moisture out from under her lashes. "Are we as insane as we seem?"

He swiped at his smile but didn't manage to wipe it away. "I'm afraid we're a matching pair." He stuck out his elbow to escort her from the room. "Mrs. Cohen, are you ready to see your new home?"

She placed her hand on his forearm, and gathering her best English accent, she replied, "Yes, Mr. Cohen, I believe I am."

They promenaded out of the courthouse, their chins lifted, nodding to those who waited in the lobby as if they were royalty, and dissolving into laughter once they hit the parking lot.

"I can't believe we just did that." Xavier leaned against an SUV.

"What? Act like snobs?" She leaned against her car, facing him. He was handsome in his button-up aqua shirt and slacks. He'd gotten a haircut and a shave for the occasion. She wanted to ask him to take a picture but felt too shy.

"No. Got married. Does it feel big to you? I think it should feel bigger."

A trickle of disappointment went down her back. This wasn't the wedding she'd thought of as a child or teenager. Heck, it wasn't the wedding she'd pictured when she was 25. But if love wasn't in the cards for her, then this situation was the best-case scenario. "I don't think it's sunk in yet."

"When do you think it will hit us?"

"Probably when we file our taxes jointly," she joked. Humor helped her hide her disappointment.

He burst out laughing. "I like you, Emily."

His words hit her like a warm blanket just out of the dryer. She wanted nothing more than to snuggle into them and get comfy. But that wasn't the kind of marriage they'd agreed to. Of course friends could say things like that—they should complement one another. Which meant she should say something back to him. "I like you too."

The air between them hummed with awareness. They both pushed off the cars at the same time, spurred into action by the sudden intensity between them. She dug into the pockets of the horrible dress for her keys.

He walked around to the driver's side of the SUV. "Do you want to follow me?"

"Yep." She dropped behind the steering wheel and slammed the door. She'd have to do better in the future not to let things get serious between them. Laughing, joking, and teasing were all on the approved list—sharing real thoughts and feelings were not.

With a shake of her head, she started the car and followed Xavier to her new home.

"CODY, SAY HI TO EMILY."

Emily smiled encouragingly at the adorable brown-haired boy with chubby cheeks and unsure posture, hovering close to Xavier. They were standing on the front porch doing an awkward meet-your-new-stepmom thing that had her wishing she'd read a book or at least an online article about how to meet your stepchild for the first time.

"Hi," he said with more confidence than she'd expected.

"You've got your father's blue eyes and his nose." She held back from tapping him with her finger. He was so cute her motherly instincts did backflips of joy.

Cody craned his neck to see around her. "Is that your bike?"

She turned to look at the driveway, where she'd parked behind Xavier. Her mountain bike was indeed attached to the rack on the truck. She'd hoped to get a job at the local ski resort this summer guiding bike tours, but that wouldn't work out now that she was a full-time mom. She could still hit the trails, though. "Yeah. I love to ride. Do you?"

"I don't know how." He dropped his chin, and her heartstrings played a sorrowful tune.

"We'll just have to teach you, then." With his little lip popping out like that, she would have offered him the whole mountain.

He lifted his face up, revealing hope. "When?"

"As soon as we can," she promised.

He grinned fully. Forget the mountain; she'd give him anything and everything.

"But not right now." Xavier put his hand on Cody's back. "We need to get Emily settled in the house first." He showed them all inside.

Emily took in the toys on the floor, the dishes on the counter, and the open popcorn bag on the coffee table spilling kernels.

"It's bad. I know." Xavier scratched his temple. "I'm not expecting you to clean this up. I thought Cody and I could work on it while you unpacked." His eyes glazed over, and she thought back to their conversation about his creative mind being somewhat chaotic.

Emily knew that look. She had a roommate who was a master mathematician, but when it came to organizing items, the best she could do was put things in piles. Usually, the piles made sense to her —categorized by shapes or colors—but they were a jumbled mess to the rest of the world. For example, she'd put shampoo bottles and spices in the same place because they were cylinders.

While Emily completely understood, it had also driven her nuts. Thankfully, he'd warned her so she wouldn't think he had pulled a fast one on her. However, she couldn't let them think that she was okay living like this. They'd have to learn some basic skills—and throw away the junk. "I can unpack in a bit. Let's do this together."

If the ticking vein on Xavier's forehead was any indication of his stress level, the fact that it disappeared at her offer to help was a good sign. "I'm not sure where to start," he admitted.

She marched over to the wall and grabbed almost-empty rubber tubs. "Let's work with two ideas: a keep pile and a donate pile." She held up each tub, indicating which one was which. "Like this toy." The rattle was obviously much too young for Cody. "I'll bet Cody hasn't used this in ages."

"I don't think he ever used it, to be honest."

"Then it goes in the donate pile." She dropped it into the box.

"Is this a Mary Poppins thing?" Xavier teased as he added two more toddler toys to the donation box.

"It's more of an Oprah thing," she joked back.

Cody dropped several books into the keep pile, then grabbed one back out and put it in the donate box. She thought about his diagnosis. Learning to bike would help him be active. Without even trying hard, she thought of another fifteen fun things to try with him.

Xavier's hand touched her lower back, and she froze. That was the first time a man had touched any part of her other than her hand since the attack. Her conscious mind knew that there wasn't a threat, but her body had different ideas. A heartbeat later, she stepped away, her pulse thundering.

"What about this?" He held up a video game. "Is it possible to donate it?"

She didn't think being close to Xavier would bother her so much, but the way her heart raced around the room left her wondering. She'd have to find some time to see the counselor and ask about her response, because it didn't make sense that she'd have that strong of a reaction to Xavier. Unless... "They'll take games, but they won't take televisions or projectors."

"Good to know." He tossed it into box.

Curious, she stepped closer to Xavier, close enough to breathe in his soapy clean scent. Her head felt light. Not in the freezing, unable-to-fight-or-yell way it had in the workout room, but in a heady fog of attraction.

Well, shoot! That could be a problem. A very big problem, considering she was now living with him in a platonic marriage for the sole purpose of raising Cody together. At least she knew her reaction wasn't a by-product of the assault. That was comforting. She'd have to squash these feelings before they grew into something more. Their purpose was Cody, and if she could stay focused on that, then she'd be able to ignore the handsome, good-smelling man who occupied the bedroom down the hall.

7

XAVIER

*N*ot wanting to overwhelm Emily on her first night, Xavier offered to do the dinner dishes and get Cody to bed.

She'd smiled gratefully. "I still have a lot of unpacking to do."

He shooed her off, thanking her again for all her help that day. Besides cleaning the front room and kitchen, the three of them had de-junked Cody's room. Emily made a rule that any toy that came with a meal had to be thrown out. Xavier was shocked that they'd filled a garbage bag. There were also baby toys that could be donated and books Cody had long since outgrown. A few items, ones Nora had bought, Xavier saved, thinking Cody would want them some day for his own kids or perhaps just to feel a connection to the woman who'd given birth to him. The stuffed blue bunny and the cream blanket with the satin edge were Xavier's memories, bought when he and Nora eagerly anticipated years of raising children together. He tucked them into his closet.

Emily didn't make a fuss about saving items—she simply made room for them in toy bins or on shelves. Her consideration of Cody's feelings, and his, made cleaning out less threatening. It also laid a solid foundation of respect that he was grateful for, as they'd need it for the hard times that were sure to come.

Xavier was no stranger to hard times in a marriage. He was an artistic spirit who forgot to pay bills if he was wrapped up in a new song. Nora wasn't always so understanding when the electricity was turned off. The first few times, she'd lit candles and called it romantic. As the pregnancy progressed, she'd become more and more upset with him—even once saying that she worried about what kind of father he would be.

Coming out of his pondering the past, he glanced about the kitchen, wondering how dusk had settled in without him noticing. Humming, he checked on Cody, who was sleeping soundly, and then turned on lights in the living room. Fresh vacuum lines filled his vision, and his whole soul breathed a sigh of relief.

It was then that he noticed the tune he hummed. A new sound. He played with a few of the notes to see if they stuck. He hadn't done that in years.

He might not be able to create order, but his muse thrived within it. Emily was like a breath of fresh air in the house—the boards and clean floors felt lighter, happier. He sucked in a breath and noticed a light floral scent. He'd noted it followed her around as she moved, and now it lingered in his home. He took another deep breath, letting her presence fill him up.

With a start, he realized he wasn't thinking of Emily as a partner or a co-parent, but as a *woman*. The kind of woman he wanted to get close to. He bolted across the floor and flipped off the lights, plunging the room into darkness so he couldn't see the vacuum lines or the remotes lined up on the coffee table according to size. He couldn't shake the flower smell, though, so he headed to his room, where he knew Emily hadn't been that day.

Once there, he sniffed, smelling nothing at all. Relaxing, he reminded himself to keep his thoughts about his wife good and proper. He changed clothes and settled into bed, mentally reaching for the melody he'd been humming earlier, but it wouldn't come. He grunted and rolled over. Maybe tomorrow he'd be able to think of music and keep Emily's scent out of his head.

8

EMILY

*E*mily hopped out of bed with a sense of purpose and joy.
Today was her first full day as a mother, and she couldn't
wait to get started. She glanced at the clock. Starting at 6 a.m. during
summer break probably wasn't going to happen. That was fine. She
could use a good yoga burn to get the day going and give her energy to
face whatever was thrown her direction.

After changing into her yoga pants and a sports bra, she rolled her
mat out on her carpet and turned on some calming music. She could
have gone outside, but she didn't want to parade past Xavier in her
yoga clothes. That felt … a little too intimate. And maybe a part of her
was still worried about the assault. Not that she thought Xavier would
assault her, but she wasn't ready for a man to look at her with
interest. Not *that* kind of interest, anyway.

After an hour of working out, she took a quick shower and dressed
in a pair of women's cargo shorts and a men's tee shirt with Bob Ross
on the front. She kind of liked the cool vibe Bob sent off, and the
phrase "You've got problems? Make them into birds" was funny even
if she felt slouchy in the baggy clothes.

Slouchy was the whole point, though she had to wonder if it was for Xavier's benefit or for her own. Xavier had made it clear he wasn't looking for romance or a physical relationship, which made her think that she could have danced around the house in a leotard and he wouldn't have paid her any mind. Therefore, the baggy clothing was for her peace of mind. She wasn't sure she wanted to dive into the psychological whys right then, so she set out to make breakfast for her new family.

The house was quiet with sleep. She glanced at the clock. It was 7:30. Hmm, maybe the smell of breakfast cooking would bring out the hibernating bears. She opened the fridge to find condiments and the leftovers from their dinner delivery. Where was the fruit? The yogurt? The veggies? For the love, where was the meat? She thought of an old Wendy's commercial where people asked, "Where's the beef?" and smiled.

She drummed her fingers on the countertop. Not even an egg. Well, she'd just have to go shopping. Xavier had given her a card for household expenses; food was definitely on that list.

Swiping her keys from the bowl by the front door, she said, "It's time to start mom-ing."

An hour and a half later, Emily staggered through the front door, half expecting to find a confused husband and starving child eagerly anticipating her return. Instead, she found the house the same way she'd left it.

Setting the bags on the counter, she headed in to check on Cody. He was asleep, his arm thrown across his face. His room was gloomy with the blinds drawn and the sun desperately trying to get in. She nudged him, but he simply rolled over and ignored her.

Maybe food would help.

Her mom would have pulled the covers off and tickled her until she was begging to get off the bed. Somehow, she didn't think that would go over well with Cody. He'd been so sweet with her yesterday, but waking up to her this morning would be a shock.

She paused at Xavier's door. She wasn't even sure what was on the other side of it, because she hadn't gone in there yesterday. He'd been a gentleman and placed her boxes outside her bedroom door, firmly drawing etiquette lines in the sand so she knew that their bedrooms were off-limits to one another. That was fine with her. It made her feel safe here. Therefore, she wouldn't—couldn't—open that door.

Food it was.

She cracked eggs, opened and closed drawers and cupboards, and pretty much raised a racket, but no one emerged. When everything was done and beautifully plated thanks to her teenage stint in a restaurant kitchen, she drummed her fingers on the counter again. How long were they planning to sleep?

She got the feeling that there wasn't much order to their lives. That was going to have to change.

She marched down to Cody's room and went right inside. "Good morning." She flipped up the blinds, flooding the room with midmorning sunlight.

Cody cried out and threw his hands over his face as if the light were going to melt his skin.

"Breakfast is ready," she chirped.

Xavier stumbled in. "Whassamatter?" He scrubbed at his face.

The sight of him in a pair of pajama bottoms and no shirt made her eyes bug out. The man wasn't an underwear model, but he had an attractive shape about him. Flat stomach. Nice rounded shoulders. And he smelled like freshly laundered sheets and sleep. Good heavens, the combination was like a blowtorch heating up her whole body. She held her breath, needing to keep Xavier out of her. "Breakfast is ready," she said all breathy and unsure—like some teenager meeting her rock star crush.

Xavier yawned and stretched his hands over his head, grabbing the doorframe. Sheesh, for a non-underwear model, he sure knew how to strike a hot pose. Emily ducked her head, trapped between wanting to stare at his long and lean body and needing air. She released the breath she'd held, doing her best not to make it look like she was gasping for air, because who does that when staring at half-naked men? Women who want the half-naked man. And she didn't *want him* want him. She just wanted him to put on a shirt so she could think.

"The coolest hours of the day are slipping away from us, and there's so much to do." She flapped her arms out to the side.

Cody ducked under his pillow.

Okay, so they were not morning people … Something had to get them moving. "We need to go bike shopping," she offered hopefully.

Cody peeked out from under his pillow. Xavier dropped his arms and groaned, leaving without a word. His door clicked shut a moment later.

Well, that was … grumpy. There hadn't been a morning in her life that her mom didn't have a fantastic attitude. Moms set the tone of the house—at least, that's what Dad said. He could be a bear at times, but Mom always managed to keep things upbeat. Emily could do that too.

"Come on, little man. Your bike is waiting out there, and breakfast is on the table." Getting colder by the second. She turned toward the dresser, cringing at the thought of rubbery eggs and the poor impression they'd make on her new stepson. The sound of water running through pipes hit her ears, and she relaxed a little knowing Xavier was at least making an effort to get the day going. She found a pair of shorts and a matching T-shirt with a shark on the front and handed them to Cody, who was sitting up. "See you in a second."

She shut the door behind her but leaned her ear against it, listening for the sound of him moving around. Sheets rustled and the mattress squeaked. A second later, another drawer opened. Good.

She took a deep breath and headed back to the kitchen. The eggs were still warm in the casserole dish. In order to keep busy, she washed her hands and created a breakfast taco for Cody, adding pico de gallo and blue cheese crumbles. He came out just as she finished, and she handed him his plate.

"What's this?"

Mom would have said, *"Let's start with a thank-you."*

Emily clamped down on her mom's advice. She needed to build up to that kind of a relationship, but she was at a loss because she didn't have another mom in her head to offer help. "It's a breakfast taco."

He sighed heavily and headed to the fridge. Curious, she watched as Cody pulled out the ketchup and doused the plate. He then went to the counter, set the plate down, climbed up on a barstool, and took the world's smallest bite.

She decided not to get into a debate about the amount of sugar in ketchup this morning, then second-guessed herself. She was here to help Cody manage his health as much as she was to teach him how to pick up after himself. Baby steps.

The kid was eating what she'd made, albeit reluctantly. She made herself a taco and sat next to him. The food was delicious. Hopefully, Xavier appreciated it more than his son did.

"What kind of biking do you want to try? Street or mountain?"

"Mountain," he said around a mouth full of food. She snagged a napkin out of the holder and wiped his chin.

"Mountain it is." Her heart leapt. She might not be teaching a gaggle of littles this summer, but she'd be able to teach this guy how to take on a trail run and come off covered in dusts and sporting a smile.

Xavier appeared, smelling like soap. Why was she so in tune with his scent? It was like her nose was drawn to him or something. *Focus on something else*, she commanded herself. She looked closer at his hair, which was still damp from the shower, and decided that wasn't a good idea either, because all she could think about was how it would feel running through her fingers.

This was getting out of hand! She should not be thinking things like this!

Say something normal.

"Breakfast is cold," she blurted.

Don't sound like a nag. For the love. Were there any brain cells inside her head? At this rate, he'd regret marrying her by noon.

XAVIER TOOK in the serving dishes and the set table. Cody had a pile of something covered in ketchup on his plate that he was slowly working his way through. He was usually famished in the morning, but he was picking at the breakfast Emily provided.

And what a wonderful breakfast it was—so good his mouth watered. He couldn't remember the last time they'd had anything other than cereal. He sat down and began filling his plate. "It looks great."

He shoveled a bite of eggs and was greeted with a mouthful of cold, rubbery things. She'd said it was cold. He should have skipped the shower and come right out, but he needed the cold water to wake him up and turn off his warm thoughts towards his wife.

"I'm just going to reheat it. I'm sure it is delicious." He bolted to the microwave, worried that if he didn't make a big enough deal about her making breakfast, she wouldn't do it again. "Where did you find all this food?" She was like an elf, all shoemaker magic—er, kitchen magic.

She chuckled. "At the store."

"What time did you get up?" The microwave dinged, and he retrieved his breakfast. The pico had melted into the eggs, and the cheese was weird little globs. He sniffed. What kind of cheese was this? Mozzarella and cheddar were the two main options in his palate. It seemed okay. He sat down again and took another bite.

"About six," she replied.

He choked. The food was too hot, and he was shocked at her answer. "Why?"

She eyed him. "Some of the best hours of the day are right after sunrise. And if you want to run or bike outside, you have to get up before the heat."

"You biked already?"

She shook her head, handing him a napkin. He self-consciously scraped it across his face, not knowing exactly where the mess was, because his stubble made it difficult to feel food on his face.

Cody set his fork down. "I'm done."

Emily frowned at his plate of ketchup soup for a second. She brightened quickly and nodded. "Please take your plate to the sink and clean it off."

He nodded.

So far, Cody had been a pretty obedient kid. Of course, he wasn't one to make waves that often. Even as a toddler, he'd rarely thrown a temper tantrum. But he didn't get that excited either, which worried Xander. Shouldn't Christmas morning be full of noise? It was usually a quiet morning around here—just like every other morning.

Xander felt the need to fill in the silence his son created. "Thank you for making breakfast. It's really good—even heated up a second time. Can we save the leftovers?"

"Um, I've never tried."

"I might just eat it all right now." He made himself another taco. "What do you think a good time would be for a kid to get up in the summer?"

She cocked her head to the side. "Seven?"

"Seven!" The word was like sandpaper on his tongue. He liked being up late, always had. And he did some of his best work in the twilight hours, necessitating sleeping in the next day.

She brushed her hand across her mouth as if wiping away a smile. "Seven-thirty, then."

He gulped down the taco. "Maybe we should ease into this a little."

"Fine. We'll try eight tomorrow and see how it goes. But if he's going to ride trails, he's going to need to be up with the sun. Some routes can take an hour or more."

He bit off his remark about how crazy that sounded. There were people in the world who loved mornings—he just hadn't met any of them. Even in his work, most people were late-nighters. That was when things got done, concerts were given, deals were made, and dinner happened. He hoped that didn't cause problems for her in the long run. That is, *IF* he was able to write a new song, and *IF* he sold it, and *IF* he had to meet with agents and managers and singers.

He had to write a song first. These two could get out the door, and he'd have the house all to himself. The blessedly clean house. The piano in his head rang with music, and he was itching to get it down on paper.

"Dad, can we get my bike now?" Cody's imploring eyes were more than he could handle.

He held back his sigh. How could he ever say no to that? Besides, getting a bike was a big deal in a kid's life. The fact that he hadn't done it before now was slightly embarrassing. "Just let me put on some shoes."

"Me too." Cody dashed to his room.

Xavier sought out Emily and locked gazes with her. They shared one of those parent looks he'd seen other couples do when their kid was adorable, and his chest warmed. He took a moment to really look at her. She had on a baggy tee and loose pants, but they couldn't hide her lean and shapely legs or her sculpted arms. She had smooth cheekbones and tiny wrinkles around her eyes. She leaned back as if his gaze was too much for her, and he turned quickly to the side.

They hurried around, doing the last-minute things that would get them out the door. He started the dishwasher, and she retrieved her purse from her room. Soon, the three of them were in the car, driving into town.

"You missed the turn. Goodwill is that way." She pointed out her window.

"Goodwill?!" He spat the word. He might be down on his luck and not sold a song in years, but that didn't mean they were destitute. Did the couches look that bad? Had she taken one look at their home and decided they were poor? "We do not need to shop at Goodwill."

She leaned into the door, glancing quickly at Cody, who was happily watching a movie in the back seat. Making a visible effort, she spoke in a singsong voice. "Tourist families buy bikes for a week and then donate them. It would be a great way to get a high-quality bike without spending a lot of money."

She *had* judged him. "It's my money, and if I want to throw it away on a bike for my kid, then I will." He'd buy the most expensive bike in the store, and then one for himself too, just to show her he could.

Emily turned toward the window. "Let's go blow some cash, then." Her tone was calm enough, but her words hit their mark. She settled deeper into her seat, as if she wished she were anywhere but in the car with him.

He was screwing this up. Not just this conversation, but the marriage thing. He'd thought just yesterday that he wanted to make sure she was happy with him. Already he'd let his pride get in the way.

A huge sense of self-loathing grew inside of him. First, for sounding like a snob. He had no issue buying secondhand—he'd practically grown up in his cousin's hand-me-downs. And second, for snapping at her, which seemed to have turned off her happiness. He'd become a wet blanket. A happiness squisher. The exact type of person he'd always hated as a kid—the adult that told the children they were being too loud when they were laughing. He didn't like that at all. "I'm sorry I got a little defensive there."

She lifted a shoulder. "If you want to pay full price, I won't object."

"I didn't mean that the way it sounded." He made an illegal U-turn and headed back the way they came. "I know I haven't kept up the house all that great—it could use new carpet and a furniture upgrade. It's not that way because I don't have the money to make the change. I just … I haven't had the desire."

She turned to him, and her forehead wrinkled with confusion. "I don't understand. Your house is fine. You don't need to change anything because I'm there."

She'd missed the point, but he wasn't sure if he could explain all the intricacies of losing a spouse and then losing yourself in the grief only to come out feeling like half of a whole person.

"Thanks." He turned in to the parking lot at Goodwill. "What I meant to say was, I haven't shopped here before, but if you think it's a good idea, then I'm willing to give it a shot."

A small smile appeared on her pretty lips. "Next time, start with that." She gave his arm a shove, and her hand lingered. Her flesh was warm against his, real, and it made him feel alive—like electricity hummed through his veins that had been quiet for too long.

He stared at the spot of contact.

"What?" She glanced down, pulling her hand away.

"I just …" Realized you're a woman? Missed the feeling of a female touch? Noticed how delicate your hands are? "Let's go." He sprang from the car, noting that the temperature outside was much cooler than it had been in the cab. Or maybe it was that Emily made his body feel warm in ways that the sunshine couldn't match.

9

EMILY

*E*mily sat in the car, stunned by Xavier's disappearing act. What was *that*? All she'd done was joke with him a little, and he'd looked at her like she was an alien species.

A thought seized her brain like the icy chill of too much ice cream on a hot summer's day. He could have thought … oh, heaven help her … he could have thought she was *flirting*!

She wasn't. Honest to Abe Lincoln, she wasn't flirting with her husband. Sure, she had a light level of attraction to him that morning, the kind that any red-blooded woman would have to a man who looked good with his shirt off and eyes heavy-lidded with sleep. And the fact that his stubble was really sexy did not mean that she was going to do something stupid—like run her fingers over it or brush her cheek against his. He was crazy if he thought she'd do something like that—or even think about it. Because she wasn't … thinking about doing any of that. They were just examples of what she wasn't going to do.

She jumped out too, the car suddenly smelling much too soapy clean—like him. She yanked the back door open and talked Cody through pausing the movie and getting out of his car seat. Xavier was back, reaching his hand out for Cody to take.

The three of them crossed the small parking lot and went inside. Cody looked at her and then reached for her hand too, smiling like he'd won a year of free Cheetos. He swung their arms back and forth, giggling.

She smiled at Xavier, sharing the moment. Her mama heart burst with the pure, sweet joy of hearing Cody giggle. They walked down the large middle aisle, headed towards the sporting goods at the back. To anyone else, they probably looked like a happy little family running errands. She sank into the feeling and emotionally rolled around in it like a kid in a mud puddle enjoying every second.

They passed another couple by the changing rooms. The woman giggled as the man kissed her neck, the love they shared as palpable as the cashmere sweater that brushed Emily's arm. Her heart panged for that kind of connection, but she adjusted her grip on Cody's hand. Being a mom was enough for her. She didn't need romantic love—it faded into a deep and abiding friendship over time anyway. She and Xavier were jumping the line and getting to the good parts early on.

"Bike!" Cody dropped both their hands and raced for the hot rod red bike on the end of the aisle. The tires still had the black spoke things from the factory, and the seat was shiny and new. There were two other bikes his size, but he wasn't interested in either of them. "This one." He climbed on and began pushing himself up and down the aisle.

"How did you know about the tourist families who donated bikes?" Xavier asked as they watched Cody scoot along.

"Huh? Oh, I spend a lot of time on the trails." She tucked a stray piece of hair behind her ear. "And I was hoping to get a job as a guide this year. They have a small staff and can afford to be picky about who they hire. I've helped several of the higher-ups and their wives recoup after knee surgery—they were ready to recommend me for the job."

"Why did you change your mind?"

She hesitated, wondering how much she should tell him. Roger had left town with his girlfriend, but the latest update Emily received from the officer over her case was that he was married with three kids and lived in Minnesota. *Married!* With a *girlfriend* who bailed him out of jail. Those poor children.

"Emily—look!" Cody whizzed by and barely managed to stop himself before hitting the shelves.

"Great job!" she cheered him on.

He looked over his shoulder, his big blue eyes glowing with pride.

She made a decision right then and there that she wasn't going to taint her new family with any part of Roger's decisions or the darkness that was in her past. "I guess I was ready for a change and ready to be a mom. Your ad spoke to me."

One cheek lifted in a lopsided smile. "People used to say that about my songs."

"Used to?" She tried to change the subject.

"They will again," he said in a way that left her wondering if he believed the words himself. "But look at you. You're already getting the hang of this mom thing."

She grinned. "Thanks. I'm already head over heels for this kid."

Xavier laughed. "He's pretty lovable."

She warmed at the depth of his laughter. It seemed to come from a well inside of him, echoing in the most delightful way. If she put her ear against his chest, she'd probably hear the rumblings of it long before he gave it sound.

The cuddly couple walked by, carrying a lamp and a throw pillow, their hands tucked into one another's back pockets.

Emily glanced at Xavier and then quickly away, lest he think she had any ideas for romance in her head. She didn't need kisses and giggles to fulfill her destiny.

Xavier put his hand on her lower back as they made their way to the checkout line. Her whole body hummed with the knowledge that it was there—the feeling that they had a connection that went beyond Cody's needs.

A nagging thought followed her to the checkout line. She might not need physical intimacy to be a mom, but she might need it to fill her soul.

10

XAVIER

A thrill of anticipation raced through Xavier as he hefted his guitar case and packed it to the front door, where they piled luggage and other items that would go up to the cabin with them. Today was their one-week anniversary as a family, and they were celebrating by going to the cabin he'd built with Nora's life insurance money. He hummed the new tune he'd started soon after the wedding and now had it memorized. All he had to do was get it on paper.

Playing the guitar again would be epic for him—one giant leap forward for the musician inside that had been buried for years.

"Do you really know how to play that thing?" Emily set her suitcase next to his and brushed her hair off her face. She wore most of it in a long braid over her shoulder, but large sections continually slipped out and covered her face. He'd struggled all morning over whether he should help her tuck them back or not, and he decided to just go for it. He reached out and tucked aside the one piece she'd missed. Her cheeks flushed a pretty pink color. They did that often— almost every time he touched her. The frequency of those touches had increased over the last week. It wasn't that he was trying to flirt with her; he had this strange but wonderful need to be near her. She never turned him away or dismissed him, which made him feel confident in a way he hadn't in a very long time.

"You'll be sick of hearing it by the time I finish one song."

Cody bounded down the hallway, wearing a swimsuit and super cape. "Let's go!"

His energy level had been higher the last couple of days. It could be because he was spending time on his bike. Fitness gurus claimed exercise gave you more energy. Or it could be because they'd had healthy meals for a solid week.

Xavier rubbed his belly, which felt smaller to him. Emily kept track of all their calories and carbs and sugars, yet he didn't feel as if they had lost flavor. If anything, he felt like he ate more, because she cooked the best foods. Cody was hesitant at each meal, but he tried most of what Emily placed in front of him.

Xavier glanced at Emily, and they shared a laugh at Cody's choice of traveling clothes. He quieted his laughter so he could hear hers. "You have a great laugh. It's like warm strawberry pie—sweet with a little zing to it."

Her hand went to her heart, giving him the impression that he'd touched her. "You have a way with words. Maybe you really are a songwriter."

He grinned. She was right: the words had come easily. Maybe this whole crazy marriage idea was going to work out better than he'd thought.

They took time loading both their vehicles. They'd be at the cabin for over a month and needed to have transportation options. Emily had plans to bike all over with Cody. Their bikes were—for lack of a manlier word—*cute* mounted on her car.

Cody opted to ride with Emily so they could plan their first adventure. His acceptance of Emily in his life was exemplary. They said kids were resilient and could adapt well. Xavier was grateful beyond belief that the transition was seamless. This whole marriage/mom/bride/wedding/life could have gone south in a hurry—and it probably would have if Xavier had picked a different woman.

Emily was perfect for him and Cody—no, just for Cody! Cody was the reason he'd gotten remarried. Cody was the one who needed help with his health. Co-dy.

Emily was *not* for Xavier.

Xavier turned out of town and began the climb up the side of the mountain. A quick check in his rearview mirror told him Emily kept up. He might have married her for Cody, but she was softening his world as well. Quick memories of the last week flipped through his head. There was Emily curled up on the couch, reading to Cody. Her laughter that brought sunshine into their home. Her general business —she was always moving, always doing, always making life better. The soft strains of harmony filled his head, accompanying the images.

He rolled down the window, letting the breeze bring him inspiration. Crisp, clean mountain air filled the cab, and he took a deep breath, filling his soul as much as his lungs. The music grew louder—no longer a whisper. A concert played in his mind, one only he could hear but would remember forever.

Xavier bounced his thumb against the steering wheel as he drove, bopping to the rhythm in his head. He pulled into the circular driveway, bumping the curb because he was distracted. He leapt from the car, unable to hold back the torrent any longer than he already had. The need to compose was so strong, it was like an uncontrolled addiction. Years of music thundered inside, shaking to be released.

He snagged his guitar from the back seat and dashed to the front door where he fumbled with his keys.

Emily parked and stepped out of the car, one leg still on the floorboard by the pedals. "What's the rush?" she called.

Xavier couldn't look at her. Interrupting the flow of inspiration could turn it off, and then he'd be stuck again. "Sorry. I have this idea. I need to get on it right away." The key turned in the lock, and he fell through the front door.

He left the two of them standing in the driveway, supremely grateful that he could trust Emily to take care of things, because he was going to be busy for hours.

It was the best feeling in the world.

EMILY STARED at the open front door. Xavier had run in so quickly, he'd forgotten to close it behind him. The cabin was larger than the house in the city. It had beautiful wood siding and a metal roof that probably roared in the rain. She'd always loved that sound. It reminded her of summer camp with her sister. Thick beams supported the front porch. Through the open door, she could see wood floors and more beams inside.

She ducked down to look at Cody. "Well, it looks like your dad is busy for a bit. Do you want to show me around?" Because she had no idea where things went. She'd like to get the groceries in the fridge. A quick tour would have been nice. She was irked that Xavier had run off, and she hoped he had a good reason. Whatever his idea was, he'd better make the most of it.

Pushing aside her irritation, she waited for Cody to unbuckle. He was in first grade now and should be doing more for himself. She'd taught him to get in and out of the car, order his food at a restaurant, and make his bed.

He scrambled out and headed to the back of the car, where he tugged on the bike wheel. "I want to ride my bike."

So far, they'd done a lot of scooting down the sidewalks. Getting him to keep his feet on the pedals was a challenge. He hadn't mastered balance yet. Practicing in the street at the house only made things more difficult. Traffic wasn't heavy, but cars sped through the residential zone like it was a state highway. At least, that's what it felt like, because she panicked every time a car drove past Cody. He was so small out there on the blacktop.

Considering Xavier had abandoned her to figure out the house on her own, she said, "I want to ride my bike too." She blew out her lips. "You know what? Let's put the groceries away, and then we'll use this big, beautiful driveway to ride. Deal?"

He grinned. "Deal." He stuck out his hand, and they shook. His mannerisms were so adorable, it was no wonder she'd give him just about anything he asked for. He'd taken to following her around the house when she was cleaning. She gave him small jobs, and he'd talk while he worked. His continual need for attention made her wonder how much he and Xavier had actually talked before she came along. Not that the two of them talked that much now—well, they both talked to her. But she didn't see a lot of interaction between them, which was something she planned to remedy.

They carried in the grocery bags. There was this weird feeling in the house, like a ghost hovered, telling her that this was not her place, that she didn't belong. She shelved things quickly, shivering as she did so. "Time to ride that bike." She pinched Cody's side, making him giggle. They hurried back out to the warm sunshine, and she soaked it up, doing her best to cast aside the strange whispers that had raised goose bumps on her arms.

Cody tugged on the bike. "I got it."

She smiled. "Let me undo the hook." With a flip, she had the rubber braces undone and helped him lift his bike up and off. Thank goodness she'd gotten a rack with three spots. Maybe one day Xavier would like to ride with them. The thought warmed her more than the sunshine did.

Instead of taking her bike down too, she decided to help Cody with his balance. He clipped his helmet in place. "Okay. I'm going to hold the handlebars to keep it steady, and I want you to keep your feet up."

He skidded to a halt and waited for her grab the bars before gingerly putting his sneakers on the pedals. She gave the bike a little push, and they were off.

After two laps, her back hurt from bending over and trying to keep him up. "I think you have it well enough. I'm going to hold onto the seat instead."

"Don't let me fall." His pudgy hands gripped the handlebar, and his lip trembled.

Emily gave him a side hug. "You got this, bud."

The bike quaked as he started.

"Pedal harder. You have to go a little faster to keep your balance."

He followed her instructions, and they were cruising around the driveway so well, she decided she could let go. She didn't tell him she was dropping back, and he continued on. Motherly pride washed over her, and she clapped her hands over her mouth to keep from cheering. Cody's concentration was the cutest thing in the whole world. He had his tongue in his cheek and his eyes on the pavement right in front of his wheel. He adjusted for every small crack and pebble.

"Look up," she instructed. Focusing on the horizon would give him better control.

He jerked his head her direction and the handlebars in the other. The whole thing happened in slow motion while Emily's mind was on fast-forward. Like a bad dream, she saw him hit the ground and knew she couldn't get there in time to stop it. The sound that came from her little guy was worse than stepping on a rusty nail.

"Cody!" She was to him so fast she didn't know how she'd gotten there. The bike lay on top of his limp form. His face was contorted and deep red, with tears that streamed down his cheeks. She removed the bike, setting it aside and then knelt next to him. "Where's it hurt?"

"My leg! My leg!" He continued to wail, and she worried he'd broken a bone or twisted his ankle. Her training kicked in, and she ran her hands over his bones and joints, not finding anything worth screaming about.

"Come on. Sit up." She helped him turn and saw a scratch on his knee. "Is this it?"

He screamed louder, which she took as a yes.

"Okay, it's a little scratch. We can get you cleaned up and riding again in no time." His voice went up a notch, making her cringe. "Buddy, what's wrong?"

Before she could get an answer, Xavier was at her side, his hand on her shoulder. Even in the chaos of the moment, she recognized the thrill that went through her system at his touch. "What happened?" he demanded.

"He scraped his knee." She kept her voice even, despite the spiky feelings poking her each time Cody wailed.

Xavier frowned deeply and scooped Cody into his arms. "*I've* got you." He turned from her and, for the second time that day, left her standing outside of the house without an invitation to go inside.

Well, she didn't need an invitation to be a mom. She loved Cody and wanted to help him feel better—even if it meant going inside the cold and empty house.

Following the sounds of sniffles, she found Xavier and Cody in the guest bathroom. Cody was on the counter, and Xavier was slathering ointment on his knee. It took less than a pea-sized amount to cover the scratch.

"I never want to ride again!" Cody swiped at the tears on his cheeks.

Emily's heart melted, and she grabbed a tissue to help clean up his face. With one hand under his chin, she gently blotted at his cheeks. "But you were doing so well. I'll bet with one more practice session, you'll have it."

"Don't push him." Xavier threw the crumpled Band-Aid wrapper into the trash. His tone said his word was final.

A part of Emily stood up and shoved words out of her mouth. "He shouldn't give up because of *one* fall. Kids scrape their knees all the time. It's part of playing."

Xavier shook his head. "It doesn't have to be." He reached for Cody, who wrapped his arms around his dad's neck and his legs around his torso and hung on. They headed out together.

Emily smacked her hand on the counter. She was getting awfully sick of being left behind. "Don't walk out on me."

Xavier stopped but didn't turn around. "Thank you for your help today. I'll be with Cody for the rest of the afternoon."

She blinked. In the week since they'd gotten married, not once had he treated her like she was the hired help. Yet here he was, dismissing her as if she were a maid who was unable to get a stain out of the carpet.

Fine. If she was just an employee, then she was taking a break. She only stopped long enough to unhook her bike and grab her helmet.

As her legs dug into climbing the mountain, the hurt hit her chest and she had to take several deep breaths. The pain wasn't a blow; it was more of a dull ache created by truth and an understanding that things weren't the way she'd thought they were. She thought she'd come to be a mom for Cody and that Xavier valued her in that role. It turned out he didn't want a partner and didn't trust her with his son.

Shoving everything deep down inside, she dug in and climbed the hill. If she pushed hard enough, maybe she could outrun this feeling.

11

XAVIER

*H*ours after the Band-Aid had been applied, Xavier sat on the couch with Cody snuggled up to his side. A cartoon cowboy sang about having friends, and the late afternoon light poured through the large bay window. Cody smiled up at him, and he gave the kid a side hug and a kiss of the head in return. He was safe. That's what was important.

And yet Xavier fumed.

Emily had left. She'd taken her bike and left without telling him where she was going, how long she'd be gone, or even goodbye. It wasn't like he needed to know where she was at every moment, but common courtesy required that they communicate these things to one another. They were married, for heaven's sake. She couldn't just take off whenever she felt like it. What if *she* fell and got hurt? The possibility made him even more angry. How was he supposed to take care of her if she ran off like a spoiled teenager who didn't get to use the car on Friday night?

He pressed into the cushions, needing to cool his jets but not knowing how to release all this energy. He could go to the home gym and lift weights, but he didn't want to leave Cody alone up here. They hadn't come to the cabin much, and he didn't want to think about why.

The music was gone too. Just as quickly as Emily left the house, the melody flew from his head. Lyrics and notes had poured out of him so quickly he could barely keep up with it until he'd heard Cody's screams. Bon Jovi had nothing on this kid. He still couldn't believe Emily could listen to him scream and want him to get back on the bike. Every part of Xavier told him to keep his son safe. Maybe she didn't have the mothering instincts he thought she did.

The front door banged open, and he craned his neck to see her pass the television room, dragging her suitcase behind her on her way to the kitchen. "I'll be right back." He pressed a kiss to Cody's head. Cody let him go without protest.

Xavier's whole body felt heavy as he approached the kitchen. There was a distance between them, and he wasn't sure how to cross it. But he did know he didn't want this all to end—it was just beginning. There had been good moments. Many more than bad.

Emily was at the sink, her head under the faucet, soaking her hair and rinsing her face with cool water. Her T-shirt clung to her skin with sweat. He blinked several times. He'd known she had a nice form, but the shape in front of him was amazing. Her slight build was accentuated by firm muscles and soft curves.

If you'll let me love you …

The lyrics danced through his head. He grabbed the countertop, his anger going from a nine to a five. No matter how justified he felt in being upset with her, no matter how much it scared him that she had disappeared, he was affected by her presence. It wasn't just her body that got to him; it was *her*. She was so calm, and somehow she filled this empty house with energy. "Hey," he said with more force than he intended. Well, he was a man, and he was upset, and he had a right to be.

She jumped, hitting her head on the faucet. "Ow!" She ripped a dish towel off the door it hung over and wrapped her hair to the side in it. Drops fell onto her shoulders and chest, soaking into the fabric. She rubbed the lump on her head tenderly. "Hi."

"Sorry," he muttered, before he realized what he'd said. "I mean about your head. Not about earlier."

Her eyebrows shot up. "Good to know. Well, you're forgiven for the bump on my head, but not for earlier." She began squeezing the moisture out of her hair.

"Wait a second." He held up a palm to keep her in place. He didn't need her running off again. "We need to lay some ground rules."

Her eyes narrowed, but it wasn't anger he saw there. It was pain—raw and unwanted, scarring and untamed. "Whatever you want—you're the lord of the castle," she snapped.

His mouth fell open. "What's that supposed to mean?"

"Nothing." She removed the damp towel, threw it in the sink, and began opening and closing drawers—with force. She stopped when she found another towel, which she also used on her hair. He'd never seen a woman do that before. Dish towels were for dishes.

He brought himself back to the subject at hand. "You can't just run off like that. Cody asked where you went, and I didn't have an answer for him."

Her face softened. "Is he okay?"

"Yeah, but I think we need to know where each other is at all times," He paused a moment, realizing how controlling that sounded. He wasn't out to run her life. He didn't need that kind of responsibility, nor did he want to suffocate her. "You know, in case of emergency."

She bumped the drawer closed with her hip. "Really? Should be easy to find me. Half the time, I'm right where you left me."

"When did I—" He stopped as he remembered coming into the house without saying a word. He'd been a horrible host. His mom would be so disappointed, and truth be told, he was disappointed in himself. But he wasn't quite ready to admit defeat. She was the one who'd *left*. "And you can't force Cody to ride his bike again."

"Then he'll grow up to be a quitter." She threw open the fridge and pulled out a yogurt.

His mouth fell open for the second time. She wasn't holding anything back. Which was … nice … but also scary. "That's not true."

"It is. If he never has to do anything hard, then he'll never learn to do hard things. Falling off a bike is a normal childhood experience. I lost half the skin off the inside of my foot once, but it didn't stop me from riding to the gas station the next day with my sister." She tore off the lid and rummaged for a spoon.

She had a sister? He shoved the curiosity aside. "My son will be his own man. Saying no now teaches him to stand up for himself."

"He'll be a man, all right—one who carries around your issues."

Xavier gaped at her. Where had his sweet wife gone, the one who read bedtime stories with voices and sound effects and made chicken and rice for dinner? "Were you a psychology major too?"

"No. Your issues are so obvious, I don't have to have a degree to pick up on them." She set the yogurt down, and her hands went to her hips. "In case you hadn't noticed, I need a shower. If you'll take a moment out of your busy schedule to tell me which room is mine, I'll be out of your hair for the rest of the night."

He opened his mouth to ask about dinner—saw the dragon breathing behind her eyes—and shut it again. "Third door on the right."

"Thanks." She took hold of the suitcase and wheeled it away.

He stormed outside to get his and Cody's things. The handles were all too hot from sitting in the car to grab on to. He left Cody's just inside his door and then went to his room.

This marriage wasn't supposed to be this hard. It was supposed to be mutually beneficial—she got to be a mom and had free room and board; he got to write music. He sat on the edge of the bed, dropping his head into his hands.

He'd be a fool if he thought any marriage was without conflict. Taking two people with different families and backgrounds and expectations and mashing them into a set of matching rings was never a recipe for bliss. It just wasn't. His first marriage had been difficult at times. Nora was demanding in her own way. She had to have the best of everything, insisted on quality even if it came with a hefty price tag, and was OCD about germs.

If he was honest, he didn't know where they would be in their relationship at this point if she hadn't died. They'd never got the chance to argue over changing diapers and how to raise their son. He'd done it all on his own.

What he needed was a dose of good advice. There was only one person he trusted when it came to relationship advice—the master of marriage. He pulled out his phone and dialed. "Hey, Dad."

"Hey there. How are things going?"

Xavier flopped back on the bed, letting his free arm fly to the side. "Not great."

Dad waited.

Xavier hesitated. "I have a question for you."

"Okay, shoot." Dad liked to point his fingers into guns when he said that. He did it all the time when he sold cars.

"Did you and Mom ever fight?"

Dad chuckled. "We sure did. Had some humdingers too."

Xavier draped his arm over his face. "I don't remember the two of you ever getting into it—or even yelling."

"Well …" It was Dad's turn to hesitate. "We had about ten years there where it was rough. I don't think your mom could stand the sight of me, and I don't blame her."

"How old was I?"

"Gosh, I don't know, five or six when it all took a left turn."

"Why'd you stay together?"

"Because we both loved you kids. And we aren't bad people; we just didn't prioritize our marriage, and it suffered."

"Huh." Had he prioritized his marriage today? He thought back to leaving Emily in the driveway, giving her the cold shoulder over Cody's knee, and yelling at her when she got home. Wow. No wonder she couldn't stand to be in the same room with him.

"Why do you ask?" His dad's voice had a knowing tone—one that said *this isn't random, spill it.*

He'd have to tell his dad about Emily eventually. Since he was feeling pretty humble over his poor actions, he decided to come clean and launched into the story. He even talked about the comeback he was going for in the music business.

Dad gave several disgruntled sighs. By his fifth one, Xavier had reached his limit. "I hate that sigh."

"You've heard it enough. You're my only child who jumps without looking below."

"I thought this through." Sort of. Not really. He'd married a woman after one interview. There had to be something wrong with him! "So what do I do?"

"Is she a horrible person?"

The question surprised Xavier. "No." She really wasn't. Yes, she'd snapped back at him and stomped around and run off, but she wasn't a bad person. She was pretty darn amazing, actually. And really, the more he thought about it, the more he realized he had behaved just as badly.

"Do you trust her with Cody?" Dad asked.

Xavier thought through the day. She'd taken care of him when he was hurt. And while he didn't agree with putting Cody right back on the bike, she had a point about teaching him to do hard things. In the end, it wasn't his mind that spoke to answer the question; it was his gut. "Yes."

"Then go apologize for being a jerk and figure out how to work together."

"What if she doesn't apologize?" *Oh, pride—thou goest before my fall.* He wished he could take back the question, because he already knew the answer, but still—how does a man eat crow?

His dad laughed. "You've been alone too long. Women are amazing creatures! They give ten times more than they ask for. She may never say the words, but she'll let you know she's happy with you in so many other ways. Trust me—Say. The. Words."

"Okay." He could do it. He would do it. For her. For Cody. For *them*. The "them" rang through his chest and his head like a gong, bringing warm, tingly sensations. He liked the idea of a *them* and an *us* and a *we* when it came to him and Emily.

"Son?" His dad's voice brought him out of the clouds and back to reality pretty quick. "Congratulations on your wedding. When your mom finds out about this, she's going to box your ears."

Xavier groaned. Of course Dad would have to tell Mom—that was how their marriage worked. Lots and lots of communication—no secrets, ever. Maybe that was a hard-earned lesson in their tough times. He'd do well to learn it before he and Emily had to go through ten tough years. "Can you buy me a couple of days?" He needed to get things back on track, to make up for his behavior. Dad was right: he'd been alone too long—become set in his ways. At first, when he was forced to parent without a partner, he'd resented it, resented Nora for dying. It was crazy, he knew that, but nevertheless he'd had to deal with those emotions.

He had to find a way to compromise to work as a partner instead of behaving like a dictator.

"I'll do my best," offered Dad.

"Thanks." They said goodbye and hung up.

Xavier took a moment to gather himself and run his hands through his hair. It was time to man up and be the type of husband Emily deserved.

12

EMILY

*E*mily loved, loved, loved her room. Painted in a soft, serene blue, it had white beadboard going three-quarters of the way up the walls, topped off with a shelf that ran the length of the room. Several knickknacks were placed along the shelf, including a bottle of pebbles, a glass jar full of pinecones, and a sign that read "The mountains are calling and I must go. ~ John Muir."

When she'd stepped inside, it felt like someone had designed the room just for her, and she'd instantly felt at home. She only wished the feeling would stick with her when she walked out the door.

Ugh! Xavier!

She carefully unpacked, not willing to make a mess of her drawers and closet just because she was mad at her husband. *Husband, ha!* More like employer who didn't pay well enough to put up with his—

Knock, knock.

There was only one person that could be, and she wasn't in the mood to talk to him right now. But she put on her big-girl panties and opened the door anyway.

Xavier stood there, his hands in his pockets and his head lowered as if expecting a blow. His shoulders rounded forward. None of the earlier combative nor defensiveness lingered on his stupid, handsome face.

"Hey." She released the doorknob and stepped back into the room, continuing to unpack.

He shuffled several feet forward but hovered near the door. "How do you like the room?"

She paused and then stacked the T-shirts on the closet shelf. "It's beautiful."

He nodded. "I thought you'd like this one the best. There are two other guest bedrooms that way." He pointed down the hall. "But this one seemed like a fit."

She nodded, noting the fact that he'd said *guest* bedrooms— indicating that she was also a guest in the house that he'd built—but decided not to pounce on the choice of words.

"I'm, uh, sorry about earlier. I shouldn't have come after you like that—about Cody."

It was a lame apology as far as she was concerned, but it was an effort on his part. She could give him credit for trying. Perhaps over time he'd get better at it. "How's his knee?"

"Fine." Xavier ducked his head. "He overreacted. I think …"

She lifted an eyebrow, clearly stating that Cody wasn't the only one who'd overreacted.

"I guess he gets that from me."

She bit back her smile. That was better. Admitting fault was one thing; taking responsibility for his actions was much better. "Probably," she agreed softly.

He ran his thumb along the doorjamb. "Soccer."

"Excuse me?" She set down the pair of flowing pants that she was going to hang up because they wouldn't stay folded.

"My parent made me play soccer all growing up." He glanced at her and then away again. "I hated playing, I stunk at it, and I thought they were wrong to put me on the team every year when I didn't want to be there. My two older brothers were superstars on the field, and I wanted to play the guitar."

She furrowed her brow, unsure where this had come from and where it was going.

"You said he'd carry my issues around, and I realized that I do have an issue with parents forcing their kids into sports. I recognize that, and that riding a bike isn't the same thing. "

"Ah." Her defensive walls thinned. She could picture Xavier, an adorable though possibly awkward teen, in a soccer uniform on the sidelines, the weight of his older siblings' success on his shoulders. He seemed to be one of those people who felt things deeper than most. He probably saw every practice and game as an injustice. Maybe he even wrote a song about it.

She could relate to parents' expectations being too big. Heck, her mother had planned her and Lexi's weddings a dozen times over. Emily had a tidal wave of disappointment coming her way, and she was an adult—able to deal with these things on a healthy emotional level. She couldn't imagine how a teenager, with all of his angst, had processed the situation.

"Xavier, thank you for sharing that with me." She stepped forward and placed a hand on his arm. "I can be sensitive to your past, but I can't let it hold Cody back." His hand twitched under hers. She reached for a compromise. "I'll tell you what. I promise not to make Cody play soccer if he doesn't want to."

He grinned for a moment and then tugged her in for a hug. He smelled of dryer sheets and soap; his body was strong and yet gentle. She sighed into him, wondering if this was what women felt like when their husbands hugged them or if it was just her and Xavier who could have this kind of chemical reaction.

"I think he should try again tomorrow. I'll come out with you guys, if you want."

She nodded against his shoulder, needing a moment to gather her wits about her. For heaven's sake, it was just a hug. However, his openness was some major progress. The walls she'd built with anger on her bike ride started to crumble in the face of his humility. She pulled back. "It's a date."

His eyes widened.

Her cheeks burned. "I didn't mean—"

"I know." He dropped his arms. "I'm going to work for a while, and then I'd like to give you a tour of the cabin."

A tour? Yes. A tour was normal, everyday, and not at all romantic. They could act like fire didn't burn between them while they went on a tour. She cocked a hip. "This is a cabin like rich people call a mansion on the beach *the lake house*."

He chuckled. "Yeah, well, I was doing pretty good for a while there, and a second home was a good investment."

She nodded. "Don't get me wrong—I like it. I might get lost, but I like it."

He smiled, and the distance between them that had seemed so large a half hour ago now shrank to mere inches. The details in the room faded to fuzzy shapes, and the colors blended together in a beautiful cocoon full of yummy sensations.

It was the kind of moment that was perfect for a make-up kiss. Where time was drawn out, the clock slowing to tick … tick … tick in the background, and the sunlight coming through the window with a golden tint.

She shook herself. "I'm going to start dinner."

Xavier backed up several steps until he was in the middle of the hallway. "'Kay. Bye." He was gone in a flash.

He'd felt that too, right? He had to. There was definitely more between them than either of them wanted to admit. His running away from her was the best action he could have taken. A romance would only complicate an already complicated situation.

XAVIER ESCAPED to the solitude of his studio. The white soundproof walls made it easy for him to block out a connection to anyone else in the house. He'd kept the doors open earlier, which was the only reason he'd heard Cody. But now he slid them shut, looking back twice to make sure they were closed tight.

He dashed across the room and snatched up a blank notebook. He had half a dozen of them open over the desk, each one a song in process. Sometimes, he went through thirty drafts before he put lyrics to music. Other times he started with a melody and the words came later. The process was never the same. If he could streamline it, he could make more money, but then his music might lose some of its individuality.

He wrote with chicken scratches, needing to get the words out more than he needed to breathe.

If it's not a date
Why is my heart beating so fast?
If there's nothing to gain
Why does hope fly through my veins?

He tossed the pen down and leaned back in his chair. Emily's slip of the tongue, calling their rendezvous tomorrow a date, had triggered the lyrics to appear. He rubbed his chest. His heart *was* beating fast. Hope was in his blood—though he wasn't sure what he hoped for.

All art came from somewhere, and it appeared that his was tied to his wife. Mark was right: in order for him to create, he had to be married. It hadn't been that way before, in college, but that was the way his muse worked now. He wasn't sure how he felt about that or what he was going to do about it.

There was a part of him, a part he was trying to ignore, that said he should try for a friendlier relationship—one that involved holding Emily close and tasting her lips.

Tasting her lips …

He grabbed a fresh notebook and got to work on a song about an epic kiss that changed the fate of a man. He might not be able to take that path in real life, but he could live it through his music.

13

EMILY

One of the benefits of the mansion-cabin was a huge deck off the back porch that faced east. All week long, Emily had been eyeing up that deck, wanting to do a sunrise yoga session listening to the early morning birds chirping and the rustling of the pine needles. There was something renewing about feeling the first rays of sunshine on her face that fed her soul.

Determined to make her dream a reality, she set her alarm for six. The men of the house wouldn't stir until seven thirty, and she'd be in the shower by then, so there was no harm in wearing her running shirt and tight pants. She slid into them, reveling in the feel of being in her element. Instead of pulling her hair back, she brushed it out and left it hanging loose. The hiking shorts and baggy T-shirts were comfortable, but she didn't feel like herself in them. This morning, she needed to feel like herself. There was this sense that she was getting lost in this house, her marriage, and being a mom.

All day long, she served Xavier and Cody—mostly Cody, because he had a bazillion questions and wanted so much attention. As much as she gave him, he continued to want more. Sitting in front of the television wasn't his normal anymore. He followed her around, happy to spray the cleaner on the mirror for her or get food from the fridge to help with dinner. He'd become her shadow. She loved every second of being with him, but she needed this time to rejuvenate—to remember who she was as a person, and to have a thought that didn't revolve around a seven-year-old.

She placed her mat under her arm and snuck out her bedroom door, through the kitchen, out the sliding glass doors, and onto the slightly chilled wood. She stretched her toes and arched her back, feeling a sense of calm that only nature could give.

She began a simple routine, building heat in her muscles and then stretching them out. Her body was fully into the exercise, but her mind was on Xavier. He was a hard man to keep out. He'd opened up to her, and she liked what she saw inside of him. His outsides weren't that bad to look at, either.

She chided herself for letting her thoughts get away from her. This session was supposed to be about re-centering.

In the next breath, she pictured them tangled in a passionate embrace. Her heart rate spiked and she lost her breathing pattern, practically feeling his hair between her fingers as she pulled him closer.

She didn't think she'd be ready for anything physical for a while, not after being assaulted. But Xavier was nothing like the man who had tried to take something from her. He was the opposite. She had the feeling that a kiss from him would be all about giving.

She settled into a standing balance pose and allowed her thoughts to drift where they may. There was no point in trying to fight the pull she felt to him when she was alone on the deck and no one would know.

She was somewhere between reality and daydreams when she felt strong hands on her hips. Her first thought was that she was getting really deep into a meditation and had conjured up the sensation. But when she put her hands over Xavier's hands and felt warm, real flesh beneath her palms, she jumped and her heart rate skyrocketed.

"Sorry." He chuckled. "I didn't mean to scare you." He didn't take his hands off of her. Which was normal, in a way. He touched her often enough throughout the day, but this felt like he was holding her.

And she liked it.

She put her hand over her quickly rising and falling chest. "I wasn't expecting you up for another forty minutes."

He put his chin on her shoulder and looked into the trees. "I may be sleepwalking—I haven't decided yet."

Ah, so he was in daydream mode too. Did he think of her this way —close and warm—when his thoughts wandered? Having him this close, feeling his breath on her neck, and hearing the contented timbre of his voice melted her knees.

She tested the level of his alertness and leaned into him, accepting his closeness, accepting him ... wanting more. Her fantasies were good, but this was amazing—so much better than anything she'd made up.

His arms slid around her, cocooning her in their warmth. They stayed that way for a few minutes, letting the sun warm their backs and cast beams into the darkness between the trees. A squirrel scampered from one tree to the other. The world was waking up, but Emily never wanted to leave this space filled with heat and longing.

Xavier was more than she had hoped for when she'd answered the *Matchmaker* ad. He was sweet and humble, strong and protective, creative and funny.

His lips brushed her shoulder. She hesitated only a moment before spinning slowly, giving him enough time to try to stop her from facing this attraction head-on.

She brought her body flush with his and closed her eyes. He smelled like dryer sheets and *him*. The morning air crackled with desire, and her lashes brushed against her cheeks.

"Emily." Xavier whispered her name; his breath was warm and minty on her lips.

A warning called out, *Don't cross this line.* They had an understanding: their marriage wasn't supposed to be a physical one. There wasn't supposed to be love. Or passion. Yet that was all that pulsed around them now, demanding to be answered.

Their lips connected in a wild display of hunger and fervency. His hands slid down her back and pulled her tighter against him. She gladly went, needing him, needing to feel like a desirable woman, needing to know she was more than the maid and the cook and the nanny. Xavier pressed kisses down her neck and back up again, telling her she was beautiful. She'd never felt so seen, so precious to another person.

When they finally pulled apart, both of them breathing heavily, she glanced up to find a raw emotion written across Xavier's face. The intensity of it took what was left of her breath away.

"I shouldn't have done that." He dropped his hands. She tilted, off-balance. "We had a deal, and I've overstepped my boundaries. Please forgive me."

Her throat tightened. "There's nothing to forgive." Because she had been a willing participant, someone who'd jumped into the kiss with both lips.

He stared past her, not seeing the forest but something from long ago. Emily wondered if it was his first wife—had they stood in this place and kissed? Was he reliving that moment with her and had instead created a new one? Did he feel guilty?

"Why don't you want a physical relationship?" She wrapped her arms around her middle, trying to protect herself from the answer and the chill that suddenly swept over her. No woman could compete with a first wife gone too soon. That wasn't the plan when she'd stepped in front of the justice of the peace. All she'd wanted was to be a mom. But that had changed over the last three weeks as she'd gotten to know Xavier. He was … more than a father.

She'd known the risk inherent in a kiss and had leapt anyway; the crash was more brutal than she'd anticipated. Hope was a dangerous thing in a marriage, she decided.

He turned from her. "It's not important. I'm sorry. I hope we can still be the good friends we've become over the past couple of weeks."

"Of course." Her response came without much thought. If she'd given it any thought, she would have said no. No, we can't be *just* friends. Not after a kiss like that; I'm going to need to do that again.

Not *want* to.

Not *like* to.

But *need* to in order to survive.

Instead of waiting for him to walk away, she headed for her room. After a quick shower, she eyed the mom clothes in the closet with disgust. Her eyes darted to the cute skirts and jeans and capris and items she felt like herself in. Instead of reaching for one of those, she grabbed a pair of camo pants and a baggy T-shirt, putting them on like a suit of armor.

Her true self was falling for Xavier, and the more she kept that part of her hidden, the better off she'd be, because a man who could undo her with a kiss was a danger to her heart.

14

EMILY

*T*he next few days were a shell made up of routine. Each morning, Emily took Cody for a bike ride. He was hesitant at first but soon learned to trust himself again. She began increasing the distance and difficulty. In another week, she'd be able to take him on dirt trails. Within a month, she'd have him ripping down greens at the resort. He'd have some awesome "What I did on my summer vacation" stories to tell.

After a ride, they'd come home and have lunch with Xavier, who'd have spent the morning in his studio. He spent a lot of time in there since the kiss. Any questions he might have had about leaving Cody in her care were gone. At least, she felt like they were. Maybe he was still keeping tabs on her, but if so, she wasn't aware of it.

Since neither she nor Xavier brought up the kiss, it had been pushed to the back burner, where it simmered quietly. She wasn't going to be the one to pull it forward, and it looked like he was happy to let it languish into oblivion.

Left to her own devices to search out a reason for his withdrawal, she'd looked all over the house for some sign that his first wife was coming between them. Oddly, there were no pictures of the woman. Which, on a different level, was strange in and of itself. Didn't they take wedding photos or something? After a day of obsessing over it, she put it on another back burner. At this rate, she was going to run out of space on the stove.

"I'll make sandwishes," said Cody.

Her heart had started doing this instant-melt thing whenever Cody did something adorable—like calling sandwiches sand*wishes*. She'd started writing them down in her journal, never wanting to forget a one.

"Okay." She opened the fridge. "Let's have turkey." She handed him the package of deli meat, the mayo, and the mustard, and then carried the pickles and lettuce to the counter. After getting the cutting board out, she retrieved the bread.

Cody laid out a piece for each of them and began assembling. She rummaged through the fridge and found carrots and cut cucumbers. After placing the milk on the table, she noted Cody's progress. "You're getting really good at that."

He grinned as he spread mayo across the bread. "Thanks."

"I'll go get your dad."

"Okay," he chirped. She ruffled his hair as she went by, noting that it was probably time for a haircut. They could go into town that afternoon. Being a mom was awesome! Cody had this smile that was hers and hers alone. He was so proud of himself for accomplishing and learning, yet he always looked at her to see if she was proud too. Her mothering heart overflowed with joy on a daily basis.

The door to Xavier's studio was open—a signal that he was all right with an interruption. There were only a couple times the door had been shut, but that was before the kiss. Now, he left the doors wide open, allowing her to glimpse his creative process at times. She'd heard him on the piano. He was skilled. But mostly she heard starts and stops, three notes put together one way and then rearranged. None of it really sounded like the songs on the radio.

She appreciated his effort to share what he was doing and tried not to feel slighted that he'd pulled away from her that morning.

Guitar music floated out of the room, and she stopped just inside the door to listen in.

Xavier had on a pair of headphones and held his guitar in his lap as he strummed. His eyes were closed, and he began to sing.

"You're so beautiful, but you can't see
The way you move is music to me."

He had a clear voice. Even when he was singing low, she could feel the way the music flowed from deep inside of him. The words themselves wound right around her heart, opening up the longing inside of her to be cherished just like that.

"Your lips so close to mine …"

She pressed her fingers to her lips. The words made them ache to be kissed again. Maybe it was the music, maybe it was the memory, but she wondered if she could really live this life she'd signed up for. Could she go a lifetime without being kissed ever again? She'd thought she could when she'd answered the ad. She'd said the assault had nothing to do with her decision, but looking back, she could see how repulsed she'd been being grabbed by the man's sweaty hands and his slurping mouth on her skin.

Not all the kisses in her life had been like that one. With Xavier's kiss, he'd reminded her that she enjoyed kissing and being kissed, physical closeness to a man, snuggling in front of a movie, all those things that came with a real relationship that she'd blocked from her memory. They were a part of her, as big of a part of her as half of a couple and a major part of who she'd always thought she'd be as a wife. She sighed gustily.

Xavier's eyes flew open in alarm.

She glanced quickly away, wishing she'd thought to step out and make herself known so she didn't surprise him. Something in his eyes said she'd interrupted a private moment. "That was beautiful—what little I heard, anyway."

"Thanks. It's not ready for scrutiny quite yet. I have a lot of refining to do." He clapped his hand on the back of his neck. For a moment, she could see him as a teenager writing his first song, not sure if it was any good but hoping it was, because he loved writing it.

"What's to scrutinize?" She lifted a shoulder, working to keep her voice light—as if she hadn't been totally moved. His uncertainty told her he needed to know his music spoke to her soul. "It turned my heart into tapioca pudding."

His head whipped around, and he stared at her for a beat before laughing. "Hang on—I think you just wrote the chorus for my next country song."

She laughed easily, grateful to be off the hook for sneaking up on him. Getting along with Xavier when he teased her was like swimming in Crystal Lake—smooth. "Don't drop my heart, my tapioca heart," she twanged to the tune of "Achy Breaky Heart," the only country song she could think of at the moment.

Xavier bobbed his head for a moment and picked out the tune on the guitar strings. "And if you drop my heart, my tapioca heart, I just might move to Spokane."

"Gag!" She threw her hands over her ears. "That's awful!"

He stood, a wicked, delicious grin on his face. "What about this?" He strummed quickly, and she recognized the tune of "Blue Moon" by Elvis Presley. "Blue moon, keep on shining. Blue moon, you'd better shine tonight—"

"That's real music." She clapped her hands. "But if you want lunch —" She paused for dramatic effect. "—*it's now or never.*"

He immediately switched to the new song she named and began singing. "It's now or never. Come feed me, my darling—"

She almost swooned when his voice dropped to the low notes.

"—a club sandwich to delight."

"Ack!" The swooning stopped and she laughed, shaking her finger at him. "You can change Billy Ray all you want, but leave Elvis alone. Now I'll never be able to listen to that song without craving deli meat."

He stowed his guitar. "My apologies to the King."

She laughed, shaking her head at their silliness. They made their way to the kitchen.

"I don't normally sing for people." Xavier gathered cups to put on the table while Cody added the final touches to their *sandwishes.*

Emily hugged herself. This was what she was after—a family. Normal days filled with activity and laughter. The sense that she mattered. Hormones faded away. This family they were building was so much more real than the bluster of attraction that threatened to haul her away. Sharing moments with these two should be enough. "Why not?"

"I freeze on stage. In the worst way."

She lifted a shoulder. His confession might have cost him something. He sounded like a cowboy saying he couldn't ride a horse. "It's too bad. You have a great voice."

"Thanks."

Xavier was real. And he was making a real effort to build a lasting friendship—just like he'd promised in his ad. He didn't have to take the time to make her laugh just now, but he did. He didn't have to make eye contact just before they bowed their heads to pray over their meal, but he did.

They dug into the food. "I think Cody and I are going into town after lunch. He needs a haircut, and we need food. This is the last of the turkey." She lifted her sandwich with three measly thin slices. Cody was fair and had divvied things equally between them.

"Let's all go. I could use a break from the studio, and that way I can help with Cody."

Emily sagged in her seat. "Thanks." She was grateful he was willing to go and help. But why, oh why did Xavier have to be so great? A week ago, she'd been angry with him for treating her like the hired help. Now, she wished he'd go back to that, because treating her like a spouse—minus the physical relationship—was excruciatingly wonderful, though it teased her that there could be more between them.

They finished up lunch and piled in Xavier's SUV to go to town. The road down the mountain was just as winding and relaxing as it had been on the way up to the cabin. She couldn't believe they'd spent a week sequestered up there, away from the rest of the world, and she hadn't felt like anything was lacking in her life except for seeing her sister. She'd need to set up a lunch date, because girl talk *had* to happen soon. An outside opinion on the status of her relationship would be greatly appreciated.

They went for haircuts first; Xavier decided he'd better get one while they were there, and he was done first. "What do you think?" The sides were shaved short and the top left long. The stylist had used gel to make it all shiny.

Emily's fingers twitched with the need to run through the length and feel the stubble on the back of his head. Oh, the torture. She swallowed her growing desire. "It looks great."

Xavier paid for the haircuts.

Cody bounded out of his seat. "I got a sucker." He held up the green Dum-Dum and grinned.

"He did so good," cooed the stylist, looking Xavier over as if he were on a menu. "I just couldn't resist giving him a treat." She flipped her long, blond hair over her shoulder and batted her lashes.

Xavier stared at the display of hair products—ignoring her open perusal of his shoulders and chest.

Feeling territorial, Emily stepped in front of Xavier, interrupting the woman's blatant flirtations. "Our little guy is the best." She combed his hair with her fingers. "Let's get going."

"Okay." Cody smiled up at her in that way that made her feel like the best mom in the whole world. "If I'm good at the store can I have another sucker?"

She laughed lightly, even though she wanted to tell the stylist that she should have asked before giving Cody a treat. He was prediabetic, and hard candy was not on his diet. But she told herself to calm down —one Dum-Dum wasn't going to send him over the edge. And after a week of daily bike rides and a couple weeks of eating healthy, his face was thinning out. She had high hopes that his next checkup would show that he was out of the danger zone. "Probably not. But we'll figure out something really good to make for dessert." She'd seen a recipe for sugar-free pudding made with almond milk that looked like it would taste pretty good.

As they walked to their car, Emily heard her name called across the parking lot. She looked up to see Charity from the PT clinic waving both arms to get her attention. She wore purple scrubs, indicating that she'd just gotten off work.

Emily waved back, a feeling of dread the size of an avocado in her stomach. She glanced at Xavier. Her life with him had been separate from her life before. Even more so now that they lived at the cabin. A collision didn't sound like a good thing.

"Oh my gosh! We've all been so worried about you." Charity hugged her tight. "No one has seen you around or heard anything. What's going on with the case?"

Emily did her best to keep a smile on her face. She'd decided not to bring all her baggage into this marriage and that Roger would not taint her little family, so she hadn't told Xavier a thing about it.

"You'll never guess what happened." Emily hopped on her toes, the picture of a woman who had the most exciting news to share. "I got married!" She held up her left hand and flashed her ring. It wasn't a large ring, but it wasn't a pin either. "I'm a full-time mom now and loving every minute of it."

Xavier cleared his throat. She ignored him. She didn't want Charity becoming chummy or sticking around too long, and she had the ability to make small chat for hours.

"Life's been so busy, I haven't had time to come visit, but I will soon." She gave Charity another hug. "I'm so glad you stopped. Bye." She turned quickly and ushered Cody into the back seat, clicking his restraints in place. All the while, she monitored Xavier. He didn't linger to talk to Charity but climbed behind the wheel.

Charity hurried into the chain salon. Emily breathed a sigh of relief.

She joined Xavier in the front seat and settled in. "I need to get some almond milk for this recipe I want to try. Will you remind me?"

He looked at her for a moment before answering. "Sure."

She prayed he wouldn't ask about the strange conversation or the *case*. In truth, she'd hardly thought about it the last couple of days. But seeing Charity again brought it all back with force. This must be what her counselor had called a *trigger*. He'd said that things or moments would bring the memory to the surface. She checked her hands. They weren't shaking—so that was a good sign.

Xavier started the car. She dug out her phone and began making a shopping list, doing her best to pretend that conversation hadn't taken place.

"Was that someone from your old job?" Xavier asked as he pulled away from a stop sign.

"Yeah." She flapped her hand dismissively. "Just an acquaintance. We didn't work that closely together."

"She seemed worried about you …" His leading statement was a question she didn't want to answer.

"Well, I quit suddenly and dropped off the face of the earth. I didn't exactly tell them I had answered your ad in the paper." She smiled, but inside she shriveled away from the lies of omission. Part of her thought she should tell him, and the other part told her to keep her mouth shut. She didn't want Xavier to see her as a victim. And the whole experience made her feel dirty. She knew she wasn't; she knew that Roger was the one with the problem and that she hadn't done anything to invite him to touch her. Still, the sense that he'd darkened a part of her lingered in the back of her mind.

"Ground turkey," she blurted. "I think we should have tacos one night this week."

Xavier nodded. "Sounds good."

She continued to focus on her phone, shutting off any more conversation that didn't revolve around groceries.

15

*X*avier pushed the cart up and down the aisles while Emily stacked it with more food than they could eat in a month. If he'd been shopping, they would have hit the frozen foods aisle and called it a day. Not Emily. She lingered in the produce, smelling melons and checking the bottom of strawberry cartons for bruised fruit. She bought organic and non-GMO items.

She was super-focused on shopping—turning it into an Olympic sport. Whatever the issue had been with her ex-coworker, she didn't want to talk about it. So why did he feel the need to push her, to uncover her secret? He should give her space to work through things. Her life before they were married was her own. But he had this feeling that there was something lingering. In the couple of weeks they'd spent together, he didn't once feel like she was dishonest with him— but she was hiding something about her last job. In his gut, he knew it wasn't anything that would jeopardize him or Cody. But it had affected Emily. And he cared about her enough to ask.

Emily picked up a bag of marshmallows and added them to the cart.

He'd seen her bristle at the sucker the hairstylist gave Cody earlier, so he had to ask, "Aren't those pure sugar?"

She smiled easily, and he was grateful she didn't get defensive. "Cody's doing great." They both smiled at him sitting in the basket, surrounded by groceries while watching a show on Xavier's phone. "I didn't like that she didn't ask first. There are tons of kids out there with food allergies and sensitivities. I think people should be more aware. I'm planning a vegetarian dinner tomorrow night; he can have some carbs after that."

Xavier agreed. "He spends so much time outside now. I think he's going to become part of the forest one of these days." Besides bike rides, they hiked and swam in the pool and played a game that included throwing the tennis ball against the garage.

She hip-bumped him. "That's the idea."

He chuckled. "We need to get body wash too—he smells like he lives in the forest." He waved his hand in front of his face and grimaced.

She laughed. "Duly noted."

They turned the corner and bumped carts with a brunette. Both women screamed like little girls and dashed around the carts to throw their arms around one another. In seconds, they were talking excitedly.

"Your hair looks great." Emily picked up a strand of the woman's hair and looked closely. "What did you do?"

"I dyed it a shade darker."

They continued to laugh and joke. Xavier enjoyed the animation on Emily's face. He caught the resemblance between the two women, the wide smiles, the apple cheeks, and the slight builds. This had to be her sister.

While he was being completely ignored, it didn't feel like Emily was doing it on purpose. She was just thrilled to be with Lexi—he'd picked up on her name between the giggles and exclamations and rapidly flowing conversations.

He'd also picked up a large dose of guilt. Obviously these two were close, and yet they hadn't spent any time together since the wedding. He and Cody had monopolized Emily's time. She'd immersed herself into their lives, and he'd done nothing to join hers.

Maybe if he had, she'd feel more comfortable telling him about her last job.

Cody looked up from the screen. "Who's that?" he asked Xavier.

Both ladies turned to look at the two of them.

"Oh my gosh!" Lexi exclaimed. "You must be the guy from the ad." She stuck out her hand, and they shook.

Xavier rolled his eyes. "I'm never going to live that down."

Emily made introductions. She laughed so easily—it was like a weight had been lifted off her shoulders. Which only added another stone to the growing pile of guilt.

Lexi folded her arms. "You know, I tried to talk her out of this whole thing."

"You should have—" Xavier put his arm around Emily's shoulders and tugged her close. "She's way out of my league." Emily fit against him—like he was made to hold her right there. Her body was warm and soft in all the right places, and he liked holding her close way too much. Before he did something he'd regret, he let her go. He shouldn't have pushed that far, but he'd wanted to look like a good husband—No! To BE a good husband to Emily.

Lexi's hand went to her heart, and she melted. "Okay, I'm still not convinced you're not an ax murderer, but that was really sweet."

He couldn't help the laugh that escaped. "You and Em are a lot alike."

"Thanks." Lexi wrinkled her nose happily. "Now let me talk to my nephew before I burst."

Emily waved her hands over Cody with a flourish. Lexi grabbed the side of the cart and asked Cody how old he was.

He glanced at both Xavier and Emily before saying. "Six."

"Goodness, that means you're reading already."

His blue eyes lit up. "I read lots."

"If I bring you a new book, will you read it to me?"

"Sure." He nodded confidently.

Xavier perked up. Maybe there was a way to make up for his blundering mistake of assuming Emily didn't have any outside interests besides him and Cody. Seriously, was his head that deep in the sand? "You're welcome at our house anytime. We'd love to have you over."

"Thanks." Lexi ruffled Cody's hair. "I'll take you up on that—especially since I want to spend some time with this guy." She reached for Emily and they hugged. "We need girl talk. I have so much to tell you."

Emily embraced her tightly before letting go. "I'll call you tonight."

"Ta-ta." Lexi wiggled her fingers, looking back at them as she walked away.

"Ta." Emily called back. The moment Lexi disappeared from view, Emily seemed to shrink into herself.

Xavier could have smacked his forehead. He had no idea how large her spirit was until he saw how much it was stifled … by him? Was this his fault?

She rubbed her hands up and down her folded arms. "I hope that was okay. I wasn't sure how much you wanted my family involved in this, and I didn't want to push them on you."

"You're apologizing to *me*?" He pointed to his chest. "I'm the one who should be begging your forgiveness. I feel like such a jerk dragging you off to the cabin, away from your friends and family. No wonder they worry I'm an ax murderer."

Emily's eyes widened. "She was kidding! She doesn't really think that. I mean, she might have before we got married, but now that she's met you, I'm sure she's changed her mind."

"That's comforting." He grabbed onto the cold cart handle and pushed them toward checkout. "Invite her up for dinner—or we'll meet her someplace. And don't feel like you have to hang out with us every night. Go do what you would normally do."

She studied him out of the corner of her eye. "I wanted to be a mom. It's a full-time gig. I knew that coming into this."

"Yeah, but it doesn't have to take over who you are." He lifted both palms. "Besides mountain biking, I'm not sure what *you* like." He was a major jerk, spending all his time in the studio and expecting her to pick up the slack. "What's your favorite movie?"

She twisted her braid around in her fingers. *"13 Going on 30."*

He shrugged. "I haven't seen it."

She giggled lightly. "It's not a guy's movie."

"Your favorite author?"

"Jane Austen."

"I've at least heard of her."

They made it to the check stand and began unloading the cart. "What's your favorite movie?" she asked.

"*Rocky*."

She paused with the celery in one hand and carrots in the other. "No way."

He nodded, keeping his head down. He hadn't told anyone that in a long time—even before Nora. She was too refined, preferring subtitled videos, and he'd been so smitten, all he'd cared about was holding her hand during the show.

"That's my dad's favorite movie."

He felt his soul smile. "Cool." Cody got into the spirit of unloading the cart and began to throw yogurts onto the conveyer belt. Xavier managed to grab one before it exploded. "Throw them to me, and I'll put them on there, okay?" They started a game of catch. He pretended to almost drop the last one, and Cody covered his mouth with his hands and laughed.

Emily planted a kiss on Cody's hair as she hefted the bag of potatoes.

"Um, speaking of parents." Xavier took the bag from her. "Mine would like to meet you."

Her jaw dropped.

"And I'd like to meet yours. I didn't think this through all the way when I placed the ad—and then I met you, and you were perfect."

Her cheeks turned a rosy pink.

He hurried to pick up the bag of almond flour. "But if we're going to be a family, then that means we should include grandparents and aunts and uncles. I mean—if you feel ready for that step. I don't want to push you."

The store clerk had her sliver head bent over her task, but her eyes darted back and forth between them. She was probably storing their odd conversation in her brain so she could relate it back to her coworkers in the break room later. Oh well, there wasn't much he could do about that, and he really wanted to know if Emily felt as close to him, trusted him, as much as he trusted her.

"I feel like we're on a train moving backward. I should have met your parents *before* we got married." She ran her fingers through her hair, moving the stray pieces off her face and tucking them behind her ear. One fell out, and he reached up and tucked it back in without thinking about what he was doing. He'd promised himself that he would maintain physical boundaries, but he'd done a lousy job of that today.

"My parents are chill," he offered. At least, Dad would be. Who knew what Mom was going to do? "You adore their grandchild, so you have something pretty big in common."

She smiled down at Cody, who had gone back to watching his movie. "I can totally see that the way to his grandma's heart is right through those chubby cheeks."

"What if I invite them out for a visit for a couple days?"

She blanched. "I'm sleeping in the guest room. Won't that seem weird?"

The checker perked up and then ducked her head quickly again.

Xavier did his best not to smile. She was getting an earful today. "I already told Dad about our arrangement."

"Great! They probably think I'm crazy." Emily dug through her purse and handed a credit card to the cashier.

"Actually, they were so hung up on my decision to marry a stranger that they didn't think about your motives." She made a face, and he chuckled. "I'm glad you're not too serious or stressed about this—it's nice to talk to you about things." He brushed her hand. "You're very easy to have a conversation with."

"You too. That could have been a lot more uncomfortable. Maybe we're getting the hang of this whole marriage thing." She took her card back and smiled at the cashier, who smiled as if she hadn't heard a word.

He took her hand as they walked out, pushing the cart with his other. "You need to know that you're probably my best friend."

She laughed. "Well, then you should probably know that I like to ride the grocery cart to the car." She let go of his hand and jumped on the bottom bar with both feet. Cody looked up, and his face brightened.

Xavier grinned. Putting one hand on either side of Emily, he broke into a run. Her laughter pealed through the parking lot, drawing stares, but he didn't care. Let them look. Let them see his beautiful wife and his happy son giggling and being silly. As his heart expanded to allow Emily deeper inside, the words of a song slammed into his thoughts.

A GIRL I can laugh with
   Who always brings a smile
   I'll give you an inch of my love
   Hoping you'll take a mile.

LOVE. Funny, that word. There was a lot attached to it when the songs he wrote were so simple. Boy meets girl. Boy is blown away by her. Boy loves her.

Simple, right? But real life wasn't a country music ballad. In real life, a man had to keep his love for a woman close to his heart, because there was more than his heart at stake. He had Cody to consider. And as he watched his son throw his arms around Emily as she lifted him from the grocery cart and then blew raspberries into his neck, making him laugh until his face turned red, he knew he couldn't mess up his marriage by falling in love with his wife. Love didn't have any guarantees—hence the other 45% of the songs he wrote that dealt with broken hearts. The only way to ensure Emily stuck around was to be her friend. That he could do—even if his whole body yelled that it wanted to hold her close and make her his 100% wife.

Shoot, there was another song idea, and he was at least an hour away from the studio.

Emily came up beside him and took the keys out of his hand. "I'll drive. You write."

"But—"

"You're in music mode." She smiled, totally at ease with his quirky mind and need to follow his muse. "It's fine. Cody will sleep, and I'll put a book on tape. Your headphones are in the side console."

His firm resolve to stay just friends seriously wavered. But he managed to wrestle it back into submission and not kiss her right there in Ted's Grocery parking lot. Barely.

Maybe he'd encourage his parents to get there sooner rather than later. Surely their presence would help him keep his thoughts about his wife in line.

16

EMILY

*E*mily gave the dining room table a critical once-over. The bright yellow table runner looked beautiful against the walnut wood, and the glass vase full of pinecones and acorns—collected by her and Cody that very morning—was a natural addition.

The game hens were in the roaster, done but staying warm. The brown rice stuffing with cranberries and thyme rested in the serving dish in a 170-degree oven. She'd prepared and chilled a Mediterranean orange salad. Cody finished putting the last popover on the bread plates. The food would be divine—she'd pulled out all the stops for her first meal with her new in-laws.

So why was she so nervous?

She and Xavier were already married—it shouldn't matter if his parents approved of her.

Except that it did.

Her mom and grandmother had never gotten along, and the tension between them blanketed every holiday and birthday party of her youth. She didn't want that for Cody.

There was a knock at the front door, followed by a squeak of the hinge and a high-pitched "Yoo-hoo!"

"Here." Cody shoved the bread basket into her stomach and took off at a run for the front door.

She smiled after him, thinking of the kid who'd rarely gotten off the couch when she'd moved in just a month ago. He was a bundle of energy now, constantly wanting to run, bike, swim, hike, and play until he zonked out.

"Grandma!" Cody's voice was so full of joy that a small bit of jealousy spiked through Emily. She quickly brushed it aside. Every kid should be that excited to see their grandparents.

She set the bread basket on one end of the table and made her way to the front entry. Xavier came from the kitchen, where he was filling the water pitcher with lemonade. He gave her hand a light tug and then let go.

His gesture was probably meant to reassure her that everything was going to be all right, but all it did was unleash the butterflies in her stomach. Every time he touched her, they went nuts, and she couldn't seem to stop it from happening. It didn't matter that she'd sat them all down and explained the situation. They thought Xavier was totally hot, and they were going to flap their wings like crazed fangirls.

She glanced down at the shapeless dress she'd chosen. It landed just above her knees and was in style with a floral print and cap sleeves. It just wasn't really her style. She would have chosen a flirty skirt and a tee with a huge necklace and bangles on her wrist. But this dress felt like a shield—though what she was shielding herself from, she wasn't sure. She had chosen to wear her hair down for the first time since she'd done yoga on the deck. She'd fought against the natural waves for years, but now she kind of liked the volume.

When she made it to the foyer, the look on Xavier's face said that he liked it too. His eyes had a smolder that lit an inferno inside her chest and a slow burn in her lower belly. Her world tipped and she stopped walking lest she trip and make a fool of herself.

Introductions were quick, considering Cody bounced around them all like a jackrabbit. Emily moved to hug Eleanor but was met with an outstretched hand and a stiff smile. "It's a pleasure to meet you."

She stumbled back and recovered quickly, giving a firm handshake in return. "The pleasure is mine." Feeling rebuffed, she offered her hand to Zayne.

He pumped her arm as if he was looking for oil. "Welcome to the family, little girl."

Little girl? She glanced at Xavier for help. He was all smiles, as if this were a normal family meeting. Maybe it was in his family—she came from a long line of huggers.

"I hope you're hungry." Even if she hadn't won them over at introductions, her dinner would do the trick.

"Oh, we had a late lunch on the road." Eleanor flapped her hand, dismissing all of Emily's hard work without even knowing it.

"Besides, it's this guy we really came to see." Zayne reached down and picked up Cody, who patted both of Zayne's cheeks.

"You should see him ride his bike." Emily forced a smile. "He's mastered the twelve-inch jump."

"Really?" Both grandparents turned to Cody for confirmation.

He pressed his lips together and nodded once.

"I'd like to see that," said Zayne.

Cody began to wiggle out of his hold. "Come on. It's in the driveway." He grabbed Eleanor's hand and tugged her back to the door.

They laughed at his enthusiasm. "I'll get his helmet. I think it's in the mudroom." Emily headed that direction before Xavier could offer to get it for her. He'd opened his mouth as if he was going to do just that, but she wasn't ready to be alone with his parents. And if she was honest, she was ticked off that she'd gone to so much work to prepare a meal just to have it swatted away.

She found the helmet and swung past the kitchen to check the hens. They'd dry out if she didn't add more chicken stock. Steam floated out when she lifted the lid. She quickly added a half cup of liquid and checked the heat settings on the rest of the dishes. Eleanor didn't know about dinner. She couldn't fault them for eating if they were hungry. She sighed heavily and headed for the driveway.

Cody clipped his helmet in place and grabbed his bike. He liked to leave it lying on the grass by the front porch. She had no problems with that. He loved running out the door and having it right there so much that she didn't see much harm in indulging him. Although, now she questioned her leniency. Would Xavier's parents think she was slacking as a mother because she hadn't taught him to take better care of his things?

Her stomach twisted. Perhaps skipping dinner was a good idea after all.

Cody did several loops around the circular drive before running up the jump and launching his bike. He landed perfectly and kept going as they applauded his skills.

"He's really taken to it," Eleanor said with amazement.

Xavier put his arm around Emily's shoulder. "That's all Emily. She rides with him every day."

She held back the desire to melt into him and place her hand on his chest. He just felt so right, so strong, so solid that she could use him to lean against tonight—and maybe until his parents left again.

"That's nice," muttered Eleanor. She glanced at Xavier's arm around Emily and glanced quickly away.

Emily smiled and stepped away from Xavier.

"Watch this!" Cody braked quickly and bounced on his front tire. They clapped and cheered. Emily felt a swelling of pride. They'd worked on that move for three days. Xavier opened his mouth, probably to tell his parents that exact thing, but she shook her head quickly, shutting him down.

A while later, when Cody needed a drink, they went inside. The hens smelled amazing, and Emily's stomach rumbled. *She* hadn't had a late lunch, and her body wanted sustenance. "It smells like dinner's ready, should we eat?"

"It smells lovely, but I'm still not hungry." Eleanor turned to Zayne. "Are you?"

"I—"

"Can we play Go Fish?" asked Cody. "It'll be funner with more people." He sniffed and swiped his nose.

"I'd love to play Go Fish." Eleanor put out her hand, and Cody used it to drag her into the living room. Zayne and Xavier followed. Emily sniffed the hallway one more time, her body telling her that if she waited much longer, there would be consequences. Determined to be gracious and kind, she followed the group into the front room.

Cody counted out cards for everyone, and they played two games.

Eleanor clapped her hands for him. "I can't believe you're growing so fast. Last time we were here, he could count one, two, three, and now he knows so much!"

"Emily reads with him every day, and he's already devouring books."

Emily smiled woodenly. She was beginning to feel like a car on the lot, with Xavier as the salesman intent on getting her out the door with this lovely couple. Zayne won the game with six sets. Cody had two. She had none.

Xavier gathered up the cards.

"The place looks nice," offered Zayne.

"That's Emily again," Xavier started.

Before he could launch into her abilities to wield a vacuum cleaner, Emily stood up, drawing everyone's attention. "Dinner will be on the table in two minutes." She took off, leaving them no room to argue with her.

She'd done a ten-mile trail run that morning, barely eaten out of nerves, and now she had to put something into her body or she would implode. In short, she was *hangry*. Which meant that she wasn't at her most gracious. Dang it, she should have eaten a roll.

In the kitchen, she stuffed a fourth of a roll in her mouth and moaned with relief. Chewing quickly, she donned oven mitts and transferred food to the table.

"I don't know. We don't usually eat this late …" said Eleanor.

What was with this woman? Was it an affront to eat Emily's cooking, or did she have some serious stomach issues? Which Emily could totally get behind and support if she knew what they were. Instead of prying, she said, with a flap of her hand, "That's okay. We'll just enjoy having you at the table. I'd love to hear some stories about when Xavier was a kid. I'm sure there's more than a few good ones."

Zayne laughed all rumbly and deep in his tummy, but Eleanor scowled. "Oh, we have stories. Xavier has a long history of making bad decisions and changing his mind slowly." She turned on her heel and left them all standing there holding her words as if they were prickly balls they didn't know where to set down.

Emily glanced at Xavier. He shrugged as if he didn't know what to do about his mom either.

Zayne recovered first. "This looks delicious. Can I help with anything?"

Emily gave him a thankful smile. "It's all ready. Please, have a seat." She motioned to the chair across from hers. She'd placed Xavier at the head of the table and Cody at the end.

A half hour later, Zayne leaned back in his seat and rubbed his belly. "That was amazing, Emily."

Emily smiled—for real this time. No more having to fake her pleasure at having Zayne around. Not only was her stomach pleasantly stuffed, but he'd shared several funny stories about Xavier as a kid. None of them involved soccer, but one did involve his first girlfriend. His bumbling attempts to leave a Valentine anonymously on her doorstep were sweet and spoke of his romantic heart. She only wished she had a right to see more of that side of him. Maybe …

Zayne pushed off from the table. "I'm going to find Eleanor and get settled in for the night."

"Want a bedtime story?" Cody asked, his face alight with hope.

"That's a great idea, champ."

The two of them wandered off to find Eleanor, leaving Emily alone with Xavier. She sighed as she stacked the dishes—one setting still sparkling clean. "That wasn't exactly the meeting we were hoping for."

Xavier reached for her hand, covering it with his own warm one. Her heart thudded so loud she was surprised the neighbors didn't call to complain. "I'm sorry. It's not you. It's not even personal. They're worried that I've screwed up my life. I could have married the heir to the English crown, and they'd be worried."

She huffed a laugh. "You do know Prince Charles is married and like 70, right?"

"What, you don't think I can get a prince?" he teased.

Her cheeks hurt from smiling. "Stop! This isn't funny."

He shook his head at her. "I like laughing with you." He picked up her hand and threaded their fingers together. The action somehow snatched all the oxygen from the room. "So this thing with my mom …"

"Yeah?" she asked, all breathy. Where was the air?

"I think it's the marriage of convenience that bothers her. I don't think she understands how well we work together as parents and friends."

His words were like a cold bucket of water dropped over her head. Friends. Convenience. Co-parenting. Nothing about love. Nothing that would validate the hammering of her pulse. His words were absolutely true, but they left her feeling empty inside. She rallied. After all, she wasn't going to tell him she was falling for him and wanted a physical relationship on top of everything he already offered. She'd seen plenty of married couples at the physical therapy clinic that couldn't laugh together. What she and Xavier had was better than fleeting attraction that would fade with time. She should be content.

"Right!" She slipped her hand from his grasp and used it to accentuate her words. "Once Eleanor sees how compatible we are as partners and co-parents, she'll relax. Can you imagine what we'd do if Cody came home with a wife?"

He shuddered dramatically. "He'll be six forever, so we won't have to worry about it."

She laughed and shoved him. "You wish." She *would* be content with this life. Here she was, talking about their son's future. She and Xavier were working together to solve this problem, just like a married couple should. This was a good life, and she should be happy. She was happy. There was just a small part of her that wanted … more.

17

XAVIER

X avier paced his bedroom, unable to climb beneath the comforter. Emily had been so upset at dinner. Oh, she masked it well, but he could see the tightness around her eyes, the forced smiles. He hoped he'd given her the assurance that things would work out with his parents.

But he just didn't know.

So he swung open the door and headed to his parents' room. He'd had his mom pick out the colors for this small suite when he'd built it, hoping they would feel welcome anytime. Now he wondered if Mom felt like she had precedence over Emily because she was here first. That just wouldn't do. No matter how much he loved and respected his mother, Emily was his wife and the first lady in his life.

He knocked on the door, and his mom answered, wearing her robe and slippers. "Hi, honey."

"Hi." The shower was running in the adjoining bathroom. "Do you want to go for a short walk?"

"In my robe?" She gathered the garment on front of her neck.

"We are in the woods. No one will see you in your robe. I'll get mine if it will make you feel better." He gestured to his cotton pajama bottoms and matching tee.

"Oh, fine. Kids these days have no sense of propriety."

"None at all," he agreed while offering his elbow for her to take. She smiled fondly at him and took his arm as they made their way out the front door. The evening air was warm and humid. The stars smattered across the sky like pebbles in a river of ink.

They walked the driveway and then took the route with the even slope, sticking to the pavement. They didn't have sidewalks up here, just a paved road and then driveways that led behind patches of trees. He'd never met any neighbors up here and only occasionally saw other cars.

Mom took a deep breath. "I love the smell up here. It's so clean."

He followed her example and noted the strong scent of pine, which made him laugh.

"What?"

"Pine-Sol."

"What?" She turned to look at him.

"It's smells like Pine-Sol. That stuff you used to use to clean floors." No wonder she felt good up here. It smelled like a clean house.

She shook her head ruefully. "I guess it does."

Now that the edge had been taken off, he was ready to face the big issue. "Listen, I wanted to clear the air about Emily."

Mom stopped walking. Her eyes narrowed and her jaw tightened. "She's not your type."

He'd considered the differences between Emily and Nora many times. They were two different types of women. Where Nora was refined and picky; Emily was fun and easy to get along with. Where Nora was formal and refined, Emily was cuddly and open.

He'd had to stop comparing them when he'd grown angry at Nora for always being so uptight. The comparisons weren't fair to either woman, and he didn't need to justify his feelings for either of them. They were their own beautiful package, and he could appreciate Nora for being the one for him at that time in his life. Had she lived, his life would be very different right now. Not worse, not better, but different. The thing that he took from all his introspection was that he was out of mourning for what he could have had. He no longer had those kinds of thoughts, no longer believed God had stolen his future when He'd called Nora home.

"I married her to be a mother to Cody." He stuffed his hands in his pockets. "Not my lover."

Mom gathered her robe around her neck again. "But the way you look at her … it's so … intimate."

"Because we share a good portion of each day together, and we're working closely to ensure Cody is taken care of. I don't know how two people can be a team and build a family without becoming intimate." The word was thick on his tongue—like forbidden candy.

Mom chewed her nail, her eyes darting back and forth across the road. "I just don't know what you want me to do. Should I throw open my arms and welcome her to the family?"

"Yes," he said without hesitation.

She scowled. "What if this sham marriage falls apart? Then what? What will happen to Cody? It's bad enough that he didn't know his mom, but to care for Emily and then have her leave?"

"Emily's not going anywhere." He bristled at her choice of words to describe his marriage. A sham! He and Emily honored their wedding vows. "I assure you our marriage is legal—there's nothing false about it."

"Marriage should be about love. What are you teaching Cody by sleeping in separate bedrooms? What will he grow up believing is a healthy relationship?"

He hadn't thought about that. Still … "He'll grow up knowing that there are two people who love him and are rooting for him to succeed in life. Two people he can count on. And!" He felt himself building up into a dither. "There are tons of married couples who don't have sex— who live separate lives and sleep in separate bedrooms. They stay together for their children—how is this different?"

"Because—" Mom threw her arms out, her face turning red. "—it is. It just is."

"Honestly, Mom, I'm a better father because Emily is here. She brings out parts of me I didn't know existed."

"Oh?" She began walking again, her pace faster than his. "And what about you? I know you, Xavier. Your soul needs love to thrive and create. It's why you stopped writing after Nora died. Your father and I talked about it for weeks, worried that you would lose everything you'd worked so hard to build."

He hunched his shoulders, not ready to tell his mom that he'd been writing nonstop since Emily came into his life. It felt like a confession of love that he didn't feel. Nor was he going to tell her how close she was to the truth. He had to sell a song, and fast. He could only guess what she'd read into that. "I had love. I can draw upon that to create."

She shook her head sadly. They reached the end of the level road and turned around. "You are so full of love it comes out of you in music. You need to be with someone who fills your reservoir. But you've chained yourself to Emily, and now she's in the way of you finding someone who will love you like that."

Chained? He hadn't felt so free in ages. "You're wrong."

Mom's lips disappeared in disapproval.

"Emily is soft, gentle, and kind when it comes to my *artistic eccentricities,* as Dad likes to call them. And when I'm—" He suddenly became self-conscious, feeling like a kid telling his mom about his first crush. "—silly, she plays along and makes me laugh. We spend a lot of time laughing." He stared off into the brush, the memories sweet.

Mom worked her mouth as if her words were a large piece of gum she couldn't get a handle on.

He patted her arm, and she closed her lips. "Come on, you need to try Emily's chocolate dump cake—it's almost sinful."

Mom didn't argue. And he hoped once she tasted the cake, she'd be open to eating Emily's food. Her refusal of dinner had hurt Emily's feelings. She hadn't said as much, but he knew she'd put her hopes into the meal—work she'd done out of the goodness of her heart.

Maybe she'd done it for him too, in an effort to make the transition with his parents smoother. That was the kind of thing she thought of. And that was why he was in love with her.

Whoa! Love?

The word was like a bass drum reverberating through his soul and making his bones tingle. He fought against the feeling, the very idea that he could actually be in love with Emily. He'd spent the last 20 minutes telling his mother they had a relationship beyond the four-letter word, so it was ridiculous to believe the thought was any more than a slip of the tongue.

He'd had love once. This didn't feel like that. He'd probably just thought the word because his Mom used it so much in their conversation.

Whatever he and Emily shared, it felt wonderful, and he intended to spend his life enjoying her laughter and writing music to accompany their story.

Love? Who needed *love* when you had what he and Emily had?

18

*T*wo nights later, Emily stood on the back deck, watching the sun filter through the thirty-foot-tall pine trees. It made beautiful patterns and sparkled like jewels on the pool. She took a deep breath, enjoying the mixture of scents that came from the forest.

Xavier joined her. His parents had left that afternoon, and he'd offered to read with Cody so she could have some time to herself. It was a sweet gesture, considering he hadn't been in the studio much while his parents were here and he could use the time to write.

"Hey." She eyed him over her shoulder as he joined her at the banister. His hair was slightly mussed, like he'd fallen asleep on the couch. She looked closer and found a pillow crease on his cheek.

His mom had been better the second day—eating meals with them and asking questions about Emily as if she truly wanted to get to know her. Emily had no idea what brought about the change, but she was grateful for it. Spending several days with a hostile houseguest would have been difficult.

"Cody crashed hard. He might sleep until tomorrow morning." Xavier's soft smile was pretty tempting.

Emily yanked her gaze away from his mouth. He had a three-day beard that caught the fading sunlight, beckoning her to run her fingers over it. She would have felt self-conscious about staring, but he was drinking her in, so she continued to study him, allowing attraction to pulse between them. It made her head feel fuzzy and her arms feel light.

"You were a superstar. Thank you for being a gracious hostess."

She relaxed into his gaze. "I don't mean to brag or anything, but dinner tonight was top notch." She'd made lasagna and homemade garlic bread. Nothing too fancy, but it came out perfect.

"Dinner. Dessert. Your sparkling conversation." He placed his hand on her neck and began kneading the tight muscles there. She hadn't realized she was so tense until he started loosening things. She moaned softly and tipped her head to the side, giving him better access to the sore spots.

"Your dad liked the cheesecake." It had tickled her that Zayne had made such a big deal about her cooking. Eleanor had eaten her slice as well, picking up every crumb.

"He took half of it home."

"I hope he shares." She rolled her neck to the other side.

"Hmmm." Xavier's lips met her sensitive skin, and she gasped. He didn't stop kneading, and she melted into his body. He'd meant to kiss her, meant to put his warm lips on her skin. Did that also mean that he was looking for more? The last time they'd kissed out here, he'd apologized. She didn't want to go through that again.

He put a hand on her hip and turned her to face him. "I should be in working, but all I could think about was coming out here to be with you."

She smiled tentatively. Hope popped up like a rabbit out of its hole, testing the air for danger. "Really?"

His eyes dropped to her lips. "I'm afraid you're becoming a distraction."

She held still, afraid she'd scare him off or bring him to his senses. Being in his arms was like stepping into a hot tub: it raised her temperature and made her feel like she was floating on bubbles. "Is that a good thing?"

"No." He breathed the word. "But I'm not sure I can stop what is happening between us. You feel this too, don't you?"

The vulnerability in his eyes overwhelmed her. "I do." She slid her hands up his arms and wrapped them around his neck.

"I'm kind of freaking out inside," he confessed, hovering above her lips.

She lifted onto her tiptoes, and her lips brushed his. "You hide it well." She pressed her lips to his again, bringing her hands forward to finally feel his stubble against her palms. It was rough and soft at the same time. Exciting and everyday. She reveled in the ability to touch him, to be close, to finally share the feelings that were crowding inside of her.

He groaned, deepening the kiss. She allowed herself to fall into the experience of being held, being lifted up on wings of desire, of being desirable.

He pulled away, breathing heavily. "I shouldn't want to kiss you. We had a deal."

"We can change it," she offered. His eyebrows climbed his forehead, making her giggle. "Do you want me to sign something?"

He tickled her side. "No."

She danced away from him. He took her hand and drew her back to his chest. She placed her palms on his shirt, soaking in the warmth of his skin as the temperatures dropped.

He pressed his forehead to hers and closed his eyes. "I'm not sure this is a good idea."

She paused. He sent two different messages, and both of them were clear. His body said that he wanted her close, wanted to kiss her again. His words told her to back away slowly before her heart was broken.

She decided to listen to the latter, because her heart hadn't steered her wrong before. She took a step back, putting distance between them. He clasped her hands to his chest, trapping her there but not pulling her close. It was like a yo-yo game for him—except there was much more at stake than a toy.

She glanced down, wondering if he was trying to keep her there or just afraid to let go. "I'm—When you figure out what you want—let me know." She turned, and her hands slipped out of his. She headed for her room, confused and feeling rejected.

The romantic inside of her cried buckets of tears. His sunset kiss had been perfect—exactly what she'd needed after a couple of hard days. She yearned for physical affection. For the first time, she realized that being a mom wasn't going to be enough for her.

But what did that mean for her marriage if Xavier wasn't willing to take things to a new level? Could she stay here without having her needs met? Without feeling fulfilled in the most important ways? When she'd taken this job, she'd thought being a mom was going to be enough. She'd planned to give and to love and to serve, but now she understood that giving and giving and giving meant she needed to fill up somewhere else. Yoga could only get her so far. She needed a man to care for her—she needed kisses and caresses.

She changed quickly and threw the covers over her body. She'd give Xavier some time to figure out his head and his heart. How long? She wasn't sure. It wasn't like she'd come to this conclusion overnight.

She could wait until her heart either broke or took flight. Either would give her an answer, but only one would be a beginning—the other an end.

19

XAVIER

Xavier woke feeling like the world's biggest heel. He was a horrible, horrible husband, kissing Emily and then telling her he'd need to think about their situation. He'd be lucky if she hadn't packed up and driven off in the night. No woman should have to put up with a wishy-washy man. He needed to march out there and just tell her how he felt.

How did he feel …?

That was a good question. He liked Emily. He was attracted to Emily. There was a huge pull to her, a draw that kept him hypnotized by her every move when they were together, and when they were apart, he thought about her constantly. But was that love?

He didn't have much to compare it to, and the sensations Emily elicited inside of him were so different from what he'd experienced with Nora that he wasn't sure. He was sure of one thing: he wasn't going to call his dad about this dilemma.

He wandered out to the dining room, the smell of cinnamon and vanilla filling the air. He'd never liked oatmeal, but Emily added all sorts of things, like walnuts and vanilla flavoring and blueberries, that made it taste nothing like the lump of goo his mom had served when he was growing up.

Cody was already at the table, his head resting on his chin.

"Hey, squirt." He sat down next to him. "Grandpa wear you out yesterday?"

Cody nodded, his eyes heavy.

Xavier laughed. "You tired?" He'd fallen asleep early the night before and still hadn't recovered.

Cody nodded and yawned wide. He held his spoon in one hand and combed through the oatmeal.

"Oh!" Emily came up short as she entered the room and saw Xavier sitting at the table. She had on a light summer dress, boxy like the rest of her clothing. But he knew that underneath it there were some beautiful curves, and he yearned to hold them close to him.

He ran his hand through his hair, knowing it was sticking straight up in the air. He should have gotten dressed before he came out. His stomach was in knots. He needed to say something brilliant. Words that were better than any song he'd written—ones that would heal a wound, build a bridge, and open doors into her heart. He had to reach into his center and shake his muse awake. Because no moment in time had felt so heavy with expectation.

Just as he opened his mouth, Cody's head hit the table with a *thunk*. They both jumped from the noise and turned to stare at him. "Code?" Xavier nudged him. He didn't lift his head.

"What in the world?" Emily rounded the table. "Is he asleep?"

Xavier brushed Cody's hair off his forehead. It was sticky with sweat, and his face was red. He cursed. "I think he passed out. He's hot."

"I'll grab the thermometer." Emily flipped directions and ran for Cody's bathroom, where they stored a first aid kit and over-the-counter meds.

Xavier picked up Cody and carried him into the front room. The familiar panic of not being able to take care of his son flooded him. He'd spent countless nights walking Cody around the house while he cried. At the time, Xavier had thought his son was mourning his mother, but after a checkup, he'd learned had Cody had acid reflux. His son had suffered needlessly for days and nights because Xavier didn't know how to care for an infant. The shame filled him again as he held his boy close.

Emily ran the thermometer across his forehead. "One-oh-three." She placed her palm on Cody's cheek. "He's burning up." She tugged Xavier toward the door. "It's time to go to the doctor."

Xavier followed after her, amazed by her calm, composure, and certainty when Cody had a fever so high. He was freaking out, wondering what could possibly be wrong with the kid. A thousand horrible scenarios plagued his thoughts.

She lined up his shoes so he could slip them on without putting Cody down, then put on her own. They were all in pajamas, but she didn't seem to care. He didn't either. What was important was Cody. She opened the back door to the car and stepped aside so he could place Cody in his seat.

"I'll sit in the back with him. You drive." She pushed him out of the way as she climbed in.

"I can sit—"

She cut him off with a slice of her hand giving him a stern look. "I haven't been to the pediatrician's office yet. Your job is to get us there safe. We're counting on you."

Purpose filled his mind. He was the driver. He was the one who would take them to help. He nodded. "I can do that."

She gave his arm a pat and shut the door. He ran around. Having a specific job to do when his heart was beating so fast was good for him.

They made good time to the pediatrician's office and were able to get in right away. Cody woke up enough to answer several questions and act grumpy. Seeing the whites of his eyes was huge for Xavier. He gripped Emily's hand as they waited for the doctor to return with test results. Cody was curled in her lap, his head tucked between her chin and shoulder. She rocked slightly.

"He's going to be okay." She stroked the side of Xavier's face.

"I know. I know." He moaned. "Okay, I don't know that. I want him to be, though. Man, I hate this feeling on my chest."

"What feeling?"

He rubbed his front. "That it should be me. I should be the sick one."

Her forehead wrinkled with confusion.

"Well, folks." Dr. Palmer wasn't one for a lot of chitchat. She swept into the room and started talking. "Cody has strep. It's attacking him pretty hard, so I want to give him a shot of antibiotics in the office and a fever reducer. We'll send you home with more for him to take every twelve hours. If he's not up in three days, I'd like to see him again."

Xavier blinked rapidly, trying to absorb all the information she threw at them.

Emily was already on her feet, holding Cody close while the doc stabbed a needle into his leg. He started to cry, and she rocked him back and forth while rubbing his back.

The doc left, and Xavier turned to Emily. "How are you so good at this?"

"Good at what?"

Cody cuddled into her as if she were the softest pillow on the planet.

"At knowing what he needs? At listening to the doctor? At staying calm?"

She smiled. "I guess it's the mom in me. I'm hyper focused on getting him better." She kissed his head. "Can you carry him back to the car? We need to stop at the pharmacy to pick up his prescription and some supplies."

He stared at her in amazement for a moment before reaching for his son. She'd taken a horrible situation and made it … manageable. They ran all the errands and got home in record time, one of them waiting in the car with Cody while the other picked up meds and liquids.

Once home, Cody sipped water at Emily's gentle insistence. They spent the rest of the day in the front room on the couch, alternating fever reducers and trying to keep Cody hydrated. By dinnertime, they were both exhausted.

Emily stretched, eyeing the waning light through the picture window. "I say we all sleep in here tonight."

Xavier smiled. "There's an air mattress in the garage."

She flushed. "Um …" She glanced around the room. Cody was on the couch, with blankets kicked every which way and his limbs thrown out to the sides. There wasn't another spot to lie down. "Where are you going to sleep?"

"I'll take the floor." He said the words quickly, not wanting her to think he planned on sharing a bed with her tonight.

Perhaps he'd spoken too quickly, because Emily slouched. Had she wanted to share the air mattress? They'd left things unsettled between them the night before, though after the day they'd had, it felt like three weeks ago that he'd held her close enough to smell her shampoo. Yet his plans to tell her how he felt, that he *liked* her, were still in the back of his head. Except *like* was such a lame word. There had to be a better way to describe his feelings. He wrote love songs, for the love of Pete! He should be able to come up with something smoother and more expressive than *I like you.*

They spent the next twenty minutes listening to the air pump whirl and finding sheets and bedding for the two of them. They also changed the sheet under Cody. He'd been sweating most of the day, and Emily said a new sheet always made her feel better when she was sick. He filed the information away—hoping he never had to use it, but ready to if she ended up as sick as Cody.

Cody stayed on the couch. His fever was still above a hundred, but it was no longer alarming. He slept better, not moaning or fidgeting. Hopefully they'd all be able to get a few hours of shut-eye.

Xavier had taken the spot next to the couch. They'd shoved the coffee table against the wall to make room for the three of them. He rolled onto his side and stared up at Emily, who was lying on her stomach on the air mattress. The lights were dimmed. Neither of them wanted to stumble around in the dark to get to the switch. In the soft, golden light, Emily's cheeks were velvety smooth and her blue eyes were an inky blue.

Feeling a connection with her that was different from the one that drew him to her lips, he whispered, "I can't tell you how much it means to me to have someone to share days like today with." He reached up and ran his fingers down her arm. "Thank you for marrying me."

Her eyes crinkled. "You're welcome. Is it weird to say how crazy happy I am to be here right now? I mean, not that I'm happy he's sick, but to be able to take care of him and love him—it means so much to me."

Xavier's heart thudded loudly, telling him that this was an amazing woman. He'd been so lucky to find her. Or maybe it wasn't luck at all. Maybe their lives had been written in the stars long before either of them knew what was headed their way. He hoped she was grateful for him. He didn't know if he'd added anything to her life—certainly not as much as she'd brought to his.

Her phone rang, and she lifted her head to look at it on the coffee table. Her eyes darkened, and she pushed up. "I need to take this." She practically ran into the next room, holding her phone to her chest without answering.

Xavier sat up and checked Cody's blankets. He wasn't trying to eavesdrop, but he caught phrases like *trial date* and *testify in court* that caught his attention.

She came back in a moment later, her face drawn.

"Is everything okay?" he asked.

"I'm fine." She stopped, leaning over the back of the couch to brush her hand across Cody's forehead. Her hair fell forward, and her eyes were bright with love for his son.

The world stopped turning, and all he could do was stare.

She glanced up at him, her eyes warming into another kind of love —one he recognized fully. It spoke to his soul, and he knew without a doubt that he didn't just like Emily—he loved her. Had since before his parents came. It just took him a while to recognize it.

"I think we should talk ..." He had so much he needed to say, wanted her to know.

"I'm exhausted." She climbed under the quilt, the air mattress squeaking. "Maybe tomorrow." She turned her back to him and settled in.

Xavier flopped onto the floor, deflated. Glancing around at the crumpled tissues and medicine bottles, he chided himself for thinking this was the right time to tell Emily he loved her. No woman wanted confessions of the heart when the guy hadn't showered in 24 hours and their sick kid coughed in the background.

Idiot!

He punched his pillow and turned onto his side. He obviously needed sleep. If only the beautiful woman lying three feet away wasn't keeping him awake.

20

EMILY

*A*ntibiotics were the bomb! Four days after finding Cody face down in his cereal, the kid was back to following Emily around the house like a shadow. An adorable shadow. Her attachment to him had tripled after nursing him through the valley of the shadow of strep. He took a long nap that morning but was a bundle of energy that wanted to help in the kitchen that afternoon. It wouldn't last, but she'd take as many smiles as she could get.

She cast a furtive glance at the messy living room. There were blankets and pillows everywhere, books left open, and empty boxes of tissues. She shook her head at the number of diet soda cans lined up on the coffee table. Her mom had always said there would be nights when she'd turn to God and caffeine to get her through—she'd had two in a row.

Her sleep cycle wasn't helped by having a hunk of a man breathing deeply within touching distance all night long. Xavier was even more handsome in his sleep, if that was even possible. The worry lines faded away and he was just him. She shouldn't have stared, but the opportunity was there, and she was totally in love with this father who kissed like a Marvel hero and had such a good heart it made her weak in the knees.

Funny, but in all her daydreams of being a mother, she'd not factored in a father. She pictured curling up with children and a good book, but their imaginary dad was out of the picture. It was like she'd thought being a wife and being a mother were two separate things. Now, she couldn't imagine parenting without Xavier.

Besides the bond that had formed between them as they'd traded off taking care of Cody, there was an underlying passion waiting to be explored. She wasn't sure she dared tap on the door for fear the fire inside would consume her.

"Are we making scones?" asked Cody as he climbed onto the barstool after washing his hands.

She shook herself out of her head. The less time she spent staring at that door, the better. Doors were meant to be opened, and she knew it. Better to step away from temptation. "Yes. Scones." She pulled an apron out of the drawer and glanced around for her diabetic cookbook. Before Cody had gotten sick, she'd made almond and coconut flour scone dough and put it in the fridge to proof. Thankfully, it had held for a few days.

"Here." Cody climbed onto the counter and slid the book out from under a stack of mail. She'd thrown days' worth of mail onto the counter and hadn't thought about it since. She really needed to get back to her routine.

"Thanks." She grinned down at him as she took the book. A sticky note marked the page and she had it open in no time, pulling ingredients from the cabinets and pantry in record time. Scones were comfort food in her house growing up, and they could all use an extra hug tonight—even in the form of fried bread.

"What's a scone?" Cody asked.

"It's fried br—" Emily cut off as the doorbell sounded. She looked at Cody. "I need to get the door—don't fall." He nodded and crossed his heart. She smiled, hurrying to the front entryway. Xavier had finally taken some time in his studio, and she didn't want him interrupted by their impromptu visitor.

She swung the door open. "Hi." She glanced over the man in a dark suit and perfectly mussed hair. He looked to be about her age and had a tense smile.

She slid her gaze to the second guy, and her eyes landed on the country music star Tyson Temple! She recognized him immediately and giggled without thinking. Oh my gosh! It was really him. From his traditional blue button-up shirt to his straw cowboy hat and two-day scruff, he was every bit the hunky man she'd admired for years. Tyson Temple was on her doorstep!

"Hi." The man in the suit held out his hand. "I'm Mark."

Mark …. Mark …? "Xavier's agent," she blurted like a fool. Holy cow. They were here officially. In all the day-to-day moments they shared, she sort of forgot that her husband knew famous people. Her hand flew to the messy bun perched on top of her head. "Please, come in. Come in." She stepped back and motioned for them to enter the house.

After Mark stepped over the threshold, Tyson tipped his hat and said, "Thank you, ma'am."

Emily barely managed to shut the door without squealing like a thirteen-year-old. She turned around just to make sure he was really standing in her house. Tyson was really here. He had on a pair of nicely worn-in jeans with his signature silver belt buckle and brown boots. She thought back to the hundreds of times she and Lexi had jammed out to his songs bemoaning the hard life of a cowboy and memorializing the love of a good woman. She'd even made out with a guy to his "Hard Life, Good Boots" song in high school. He was only five years older than she was, but fame had come early in his life due to his caramel voice and delicious blue eyes.

His age had made him seem accessible to the girls in her group. Any one of them could be swept off their feet by him when they went off to college or scored backstage passes. The daydreams were within their grasp.

The men stared back at her expectantly.

She suddenly realized they weren't here to see her. "I'll, um, find Xavier and let him know you're here." She was about to invite them into the living room when her mind flashed to the mess that awaited them. Why hadn't she cleaned?

She knocked and rushed into the studio, breaking one of her unspoken rules to not disturb Xavier when he was deep in his creative process.

"Why didn't you tell me Tyson Temple was coming today?" she hissed, glancing over her shoulder to make sure she wasn't overheard. "He's in the entryway." She jabbed her finger in that direction several times.

Xavier jumped to his feet and glanced down at his sweats. "I totally forgot." He dashed out the door and to his bedroom. "Can you entertain him for a minute?"

She moaned, following after him. "The house is a wreck."

"He's a good guy. He won't say anything." Xavier said.

"Men!" She threw her hands in the air. "It's not about him saying anything—it's about me *knowing* how bad our place looks. A guest feels more comfortable in a clean house, and the only clean space is the kitchen."

"Then take them in there."

"Gah!" She threw her hands up. Entertaining a music legend in her kitchen wasn't her first choice, but she'd have to make do. "Okay ..."

Xavier ripped off his shirt and threw it in the hamper. Her mind went blank, and she stared at the amazing-ness that was his body. He worked out, but not excessively—he was lucky to get in a couple sessions a week. Apparently, he was just blessed with the kind of genes that sculpted nicely.

She gulped.

He hooked his thumbs inside his sweats, ready to shove them to the floor, and stopped abruptly, making eye contact with her. She flushed from the bottoms of her feet all the way up to her roots. He'd totally caught her checking him out.

"Hurry," she whispered, shutting the door as she backed out. On the other side, she leaned against the wood, placed her hand over her heart, and tried to breathe normally.

That man had serious hotness issues. How was she supposed to keep the image of him shirtless from filtering in every minute of every day?

She heard something hit the kitchen floor and took off at a run. Cody had knocked over the barstool in his efforts to climb down. His legs dangled as he hung over the edge. She rushed in and lifted him up. "I told you to *not* fall," she teased. No harm, no foul.

Ahem.

She turned around, still holding Cody against her stomach, his arms up at funny angles.

Mark and Tyson smiled. "Need some help?" asked Mark.

She took a moment to consider her options. Being the fabulous and sophisticated wife of a hit songwriter had gone out the window the moment she fangirled at the front door. Better to go with who she was and hope they were cool with that. "Sure." She handed Cody to Mark, who threw him over his shoulder and headed for the front room. "While you're in there, can you fold a few blankets?" She mentally slammed her hand over her mouth to stop herself from saying stupid things. Who asked their agent to fold blankets?

"I'm on it," Mark called back.

She sagged against the counter before realizing she was now alone in a room with her high school/college never-going-to-happen-crush. "Um, how are you at frying scones?"

He blinked once, and a slow, sultry smile spread across his lips. "I guess I'm as good as the next guy."

If he'd given her that smile six years ago, she would have melted into a puddle of goo right there. As handsome as Tyson was, he didn't stir up a belly full of butterflies or make her want to watch him do laundry. She gave him another once-over and decided he was just a man who could sing pretty. And he was here to buy a song from her husband—hopefully. Might as well make him feel like one of the family.

She nodded and pulled a pan out from under the stove. "You're hired. Oil is in the cupboard next to the fridge."

He crossed the kitchen, tugging on one of her apron strings. "Do I get one of those?"

She laughed, feeling more at ease. "I think we can arrange that." She retrieved a plain white apron that went well with his shirt and tossed it to him. He caught it with one hand as he poured oil into the warming pan with the other. She got the dough from the fridge and sprinkled almond flour on the counter. They worked in silence for a moment. Cody laughed in the other room, and she smiled.

What was taking Xavier so long? And what was she supposed to say to a man who was a legend?

"Cody's a cute kid," Tyson offered.

She relaxed into her task of cutting dough into triangles. "Thanks. He had a rough week—strep." She realized what strep could mean to a man who made his living with his vocal cords. "Don't worry, though. He's been on an antibiotic for four days. He's not contagious."

Tyson waved off her concern. "My nieces and nephews pass around enough germs to infect a whole concert hall. I'm fine."

She breathed out, and her shoulders slumped. "So what's it like, touring all over the world and having billions of women use your face as wallpaper on their phones?"

He laughed and stepped back so she could drop dough into the oil. "It's overwhelming at times. Definity surreal. I'm just a country boy at heart, and I need quiet nights on the ranch with my family to recharge."

She handed him a pair of tongs. "Flip them when they brown on the bottom."

A small line appeared between his eyebrows as he studied the scones. "What about you?"

She blinked. "Me?"

"Yeah—what do you do?"

"I'm a mom," she replied automatically. "I used to be a physical therapist and a fitness coach."

"Sounds like a busy life."

She nodded. "The best kind of busy."

"My sister would say the same thing."

Emily wondered at the ease to their conversation. Lexi was going to freak out when she told her she'd spent an evening making scones with Tyson and discussing raising children. "How many kids does she have?"

"Six under nine."

"Okay, she's officially my new hero." Cody wore her out, and he was just one kid!

He laughed as he carefully flipped over the first batch of dough. They were golden brown and beautiful.

"Your fans will be happy to hear you're accomplished in the kitchen," she teased.

He waved the tongs and pumped his eyebrows. "I'll wow them all with my deep-frying skills."

She was giggling when Xavier walked in, freshly showered and smelling clean and yummy. He looked back and forth between the two of them. "What's going on?" Hs voice had a jealous edge to it. She hadn't expected that from him. But she liked it.

"We're making dinner." She pointed to the fridge. "Can you find the fruit?"

Xavier moved to the fridge. "Hey, Tyson." They shook hands. "It's good to see you again."

"You too." Tyson pulled out a finished scone and set it on the paper towel-covered plate Emily offered.

"Again?" Emily asked, quirking her eyebrow.

Xavier nodded. "We used to work together a lot."

Tyson pointed the tongues at Xavier. "He wrote 'Hard Life, Good Boots.'"

Emily dropped the dough in her hands. It landed with a puff of flour. "Shut the front door." Her face flushed with the memory of kisses in Bobby Tom's living room. To think she'd swooned over Xavier's words! That was just … mind-boggling. He couldn't have been much older than Tyson at the time. It seemed success had come early to both of them.

More importantly, though, she realized that Xavier had been in her heart long before she'd ever met him. Tyson might have added caramel to the song, but the lyrics were all chocolate and Xavier. Her insides were antsy. She'd thought she could wait for him to make up his mind, but the waiting was killing her, because all she wanted to do was fall into his arms and make out to that song! If he started singing? She'd totally swoon.

Mark came in, carrying Cody over one shoulder like a sack of potatoes. "Did someone order a kid?"

Xavier grinned and reached for Cody. "Nope. But we'll take him anyway."

"Hey!" Cody scowled, making them all chuckle.

With everyone's help, dinner was on the table in record time and they dug in. Tyson was easy to talk to. He wasn't lying when he said he was just a country boy. He had great stories of days and nights on his family's cattle ranch. Cody was enthralled with the whole idea of riding horses and rustling cattle.

The evening was going well. They hadn't said a word about music, though, and Emily started to worry. Selling a song hung heavy on Xavier's shoulders. He needed this win—she could see it in the way he'd thrown himself into writing music lately. The songs came to him at random moments, and he'd trot off to note them down. She wanted this for him. Wanted it more than she'd ever wanted anything for herself.

21

XAVIER

$\mathcal{X}$avier had a hard time getting his scones down. Every time he looked up from his plate, Tyson was looking at Emily like she'd hung the moon and the stars and was personally responsible for electricity and moving pictures too.

No guy had a right to look at his wife that way.

He mentally stuttered to a stop and stared at his plate. Yes, Emily was his wife, but he didn't have a right to possess her—not like some over-egoed macho man who insisted on being the center of a woman's world just because he'd put a ring on her finger.

But still … there were boundaries a guy should keep around another man's wife. He stabbed at a strawberry and chewed it ferociously. He should be talking about his latest song, the one he was sure Tyson would want to headline his new album. And then there were the two singles that were chart-toppers. He could feel it in his bones, had a sixth sense about these things, and he had never been wrong before.

He couldn't focus when Emily laughed breathlessly at Tyson's stupid jokes. What was wrong with her? She wasn't flirting. She wasn't sending out *I'm available* vibes. And she worked to include everyone, even Cody, in the conversation. In short, she was being an excellent hostess.

He wished she'd knock it off.

Tyson didn't need one more reason to smile at her. He could obviously see Emily's charms. She was an excellent mother, an active listener, and a great cook. Tyson would be stupid not to follow her around the room with his eyes.

When she got up to clear the table, Xavier jumped in to help so that Tyson wouldn't follow her into the kitchen. They were a team, and he wanted to show it to everyone in the room. Including Mark, who had kept his eyes to himself, though he'd been quiet throughout the meal.

Tyson turned in his seat to track Emily's movements as she took dirty plates to the counter.

Xavier glared at him.

Tyson said, "You guys should come down to Texas for a weekend. We'll teach you to rope and ride." He rubbed Cody's head, messing up his already messy hair.

"Can we, Dad?" Cody begged.

Xavier glanced at Emily, hoping she'd come up with a reason not to go—that school was starting soon would work. Or that she was allergic to horses. Anything.

Her face lit up. "I'd love that. I haven't been on a horse for years." She reached for the pitcher of orange juice. Tyson got to it first and handed it to her. "Thanks." She graced him with one of her genuine smiles, which made Xavier want to kick them out of the house. He took deep breaths. If he'd just told Emily he loved her and she'd said it back, then he'd feel better—more secure in his marriage. He just didn't know if she was looking at Tyson and thinking, *I could have had this guy?*

"You're welcome. What can I do to help?" Tyson went to stand.

Xavier couldn't take much more of this. "Why don't we go into the studio and I can show you guys what I've been working on?"

Mark gave him a look of relief. "That sounds great." The poor guy probably thought they'd been stalling because Xavier didn't have anything ready. He was in for a big surprise.

"Are you sure you don't want help with the dishes?" Tyson asked Emily.

Xavier scowled. The guy was making him look bad.

Emily shooed them out of the room. "I have all the help I need. Cody is excellent at loading the dishwasher."

Cody let out a groan.

"Come on, pumpkin. You've been faking sick for too long," she teased him.

Cody gasped. "Faking?"

Emily's laugh followed them down that hallway. Xavier wished he could stay with them, that he could bottle the sense of family Emily created so easily. He also wanted to bottle Emily up and keep her all to himself. He'd never felt like that with Nora. Being married to her was like being tied to the wind. A sudden understanding of that situation hit him like a falling piano. He'd never felt safe with Nora—never felt like she loved him as much as he loved her.

The feelings he had with Emily were so different. Being married to her was easy—almost effortless. Probably because there weren't romantic expectations. Yet there was romance in their marriage—and attraction. The way she'd looked at him in his room that afternoon had left his head spinning. He could have kissed her right then, was about to, but she'd shut the door before he had a chance to act on his desires.

If only the shower had washed away the need to kiss her, to finally let her know that he liked her as more than the mother of his child. That he liked her as a woman.

As gifted as he was at writing lyrics, he still couldn't wrap his head around the words that would express the boom-boom in his chest when he saw her for the first time each morning.

Mark clapped his hands together and rubbed his palms, startling Xavier out of his own head. "I can't wait to hear what you've got."

Tyson glanced around the room. "Do you have a guitar for me?"

Xavier looked at the space through his eyes. The open notebooks—

one per song—were scattered on every surface. Guitar picks littered the carpet behind the desk like glitter. The piano was covered in sheet music. He suddenly understood Emily's frustration with him earlier. The only way to get over the embarrassment was to act like he wasn't embarrassed. The old adage "fake it till you make it" came to mind.

"Of course." Xavier went to the closet and pulled out a beat-up black case. Back in the day, when he and Tyson were young and idealistic, they'd jam together. The creative synergy that happened was incredible. He'd forgotten that feeling and was suddenly excited to find it again. He handed Tyson the acoustic guitar.

Tyson grinned. "You still have Bessie?"

"You don't ever throw out a classic." Xavier returned the smile. His fingers tingled, ready to play. He felt like himself again—like he could tap into the source of inspiration as easily as slipping into his favorite pair of cowboy boots. It made him feel alive. Almost as alive as kissing Emily had. He'd like to do that again, like to hold her close and breathe in her delicious scent, drink in her lips.

Tyson strummed and then tightened the A string. "Let's hear what you've got."

Pushing away thoughts of making out with his wife, Xavier picked up his Gibson and thumbed the strings before finding a pick. "This one is upbeat and kind of—" He paused to think of the moment when Emily had inspired the lyrics and tone. "—sassy." He ripped into the melody and sang, "You cock your hip at me and I know trouble's comin' my way."

Mark bobbed his head and bounced his knee. Tyson picked up the tune on the second verse and played along, adding a riff. He'd eventually bring his twang and deeper voice to the melody, making women all over the world swoon. As long as Emily wasn't one of them, he and Tyson could stay friends.

They played for another three hours, working through about half the songs Xavier had written since marrying Emily. He'd saved a couple that were too close to his heart to share with the world, but he put his best stuff out there for this meeting. He wanted the comeback even more than before. He wanted to prove to Emily that he was a guy she could be proud of—that he could bring home the bacon.

Mark pushed to his feet. "Guys, I know you can play all night, but we've got to catch a plane in the morning." He wasn't as worn out as he claimed, but he wanted to end on a high note. Xavier had seen him do this before.

Tyson set Bessie back in the red velvet lining and carefully shut the lid. "It's been a long time, but you've still got it, man." He shook Xavier's hand. "I'm going to sit down with my manager to talk about the new album this week."

Xavier set his guitar in the stand. He wasn't sure what to make of Tyson's statement. Even though there was a compliment in there, it wasn't an outright offer for any of the songs they'd gone over. "I look forward to hearing from you."

"You bet." Tyson led the way out. "Tell Emily thank you for dinner."

"Will do," Xavier promised. Though he'd downplay it and make sure she knew that he was more grateful than the hot rod singer.

Mark gave him a silent thumbs-up and a wink before following. That was a good sign. Xavier let out a breath.

As soon as the door shut, Emily was there. She'd changed into a pair of plaid pajamas and an oversized T-shirt. Her hair was piled on top of her head in a messy bun. And she'd never looked more beautiful. "How'd it go?" Her blue eyes held a note of vulnerability that he realized was for him. She wanted him to sell a song. Not because she wanted to buy a new couch or take them on a European vacation. No. She wanted this because he wanted this. Her hope and support undid his fortitude.

He crossed the room in four long strides and swept her into his arms. "Good."

She gasped in surprise, the sound only adding to his need for her. He kissed her. She held still for a moment and then softened in his hold, molded her body to his. He deepened the kiss, and something otherworldly happened: a crescendo of emotions and pent-up need with violins climbing higher and faster and cellos thrumming along and—at the end of the kiss—a smashing of cymbals.

"Don't apologize," she whispered, putting her finger over his lips.

He could kick himself for backing away last time. He wasn't dumb enough to make that mistake again. "I wasn't going to."

"Good." She kissed him softly. "Good night."

"Night."

She slipped out of his arms and out of the room. Xavier watched her go, wondering how his life had gotten so amazing in such a short amount of time. One ad in the paper was all it took. Well, one ad and a huge leap of faith.

He held still, the beginnings of a song off in the distance but getting closer. Closing his eyes, he concentrated on the feel of Emily's lips against his, and the melody appeared. At the desk once again, he wrote the song of their kiss.

22

EMILY

"*I*'m in love and I don't care who knows it." Emily threw her arms out to the sides and spun in a circle. She threw her head back and took in the bright blue sky and one white fluffy cloud. "It's such a beautiful day."

Lexi licked her ice cream. "I may not be in love, but with chocolate, I can agree that it's a beautiful day." She lifted the cone in salute.

Emily had made breakfast for her guys, like usual. Cody was wiped out from staying up late the night before with Tyson and Mark, and he was grouchy, so she felt kind of bad leaving him to meet up with her sister. But she and Lexi had had lunch, ice cream, and girl talk planned for over a week, so she couldn't cancel.

They sat on a bench to work on their individual ice cream creations. The street vendor had limited options, vanilla or chocolate, but he mixed in all sorts of wonderful things. Emily had peanut butter cups, hot fudge, caramel, and walnuts. Lexi had gone with her usual, chocolate with Butterfinger chunks.

"How'd he tell you he's in love with you?" asked Lexi.

Emily made slow swirls in her ice cream with the spoon. "He hasn't."

"But you just said you guys kissed and the earth moved beneath your feet."

"We, umm, haven't exactly said those words."

Lexi pointed at her and narrowed her eyes. "You're telling me. You two are *married*. You're raising a kid *together*. And you're *kissing*. And you don't say *I love you?*"

"Not to each other."

"That's whack."

Emily giggled. "I know. It's not normal. Who's to say what normal family looks like these days?" The sun filtered through the leaves above them. Children laughed on the playground far enough away that the screams were muted. Emily let out a contented sigh. "I finally have the family I always wanted. I'm not going to lie, it's an amazing feeling."

"I hate to rain on your parade, but you still haven't told Mom and Dad." Lexi took a huge bite of ice cream and grimaced. "Cold," she managed to get out as she rubbed her temples.

"I'm calling them right now." She dialed her parents and grinned when her dad picked up. They said hello, and she jumped right in, feeling invincible wrapped in a cape of love. "So, I got married."

Her proclamation was met with silence. Dad finally said, "You're joking, right?"

"I'm not. Dad, it's a long story. Can you get Mom so I only have to tell it once?" She grinned at Lexi, who was taking another huge bite. The girl had a weakness for sweets that was going to freeze her brain. Right on cue, she rubbed her temples again.

"Hey, sweetheart." Mom's melodic voice filled the line. "Your dad is pulling my leg. He said you got married."

"I did." She wasn't at all repentant, although she should be. She'd made a huge decision and not included her parents. That wasn't like her. She needed to make it up to them. "I'm calling to invite you to meet my husband and …" She sucked in a breath. "My son."

"Honey? *What* have you been up to?"

She rolled her eyes at herself. Lexi lifted one brow in question. "They think I got pregnant," she whispered.

Lexi snorted and covered her mouth with a napkin.

"It's nothing like that. Cody is six. He's smart and sweet and seriously funny. You're going to love him."

Lexi leaned over so she was closer to the phone. "I already do."

"Is Lexi there?" demanded Dad.

"Right here," Emily confirmed.

"Put her on."

She rolled her eyes again. "They want to talk to you."

Lexi took the phone.

"You let her get married?" Dad shouted through the line.

Emily pulled her lips back into a grimace. His bellow could be heard all the way over at the playground.

Lexi mimicked her face. "Dad, it's cool. Xavier is a great guy. The best. And Cody really is a gem. Don't be mad until you meet them."

"I'm not mad!" he yelled. "I'm shocked you girls would hide something like this from us. You're the big sister; you're supposed to watch out for her."

She coughed. "You get that she's an adult right?"

"Lexi," he warned.

She shook her head, making her hair flip. "I'm not going to get yelled at for something she did. If you want to yell at me, do it for maxing out my credit card on new skis."

She handed the phone back to Emily and stood up. "Thank you." She air-kissed Emily's cheek. "I was looking for an opportunity to tell him about that, and compared to your elopement, I look pretty good right now. Toodles." She wiggled her fingers. "I have to get back to work."

Emily smirked at her and waved her fingers too. "Toodles." She put the phone back up to her ear. "Dad?"

"Dad's sitting in front of the freezer," Mom answered.

Emily blanched. Dad would open the freezer and stick his face in to cool off when he was upset. She could count on two fingers the number of times he'd done that because of her. Lexi had probably made him take a freezer time-out a dozen times growing up. Mom had been more level-headed, especially when it came to matters of the heart.

Mom sighed. "Why don't you start over? I'd like to hear this story."

"It's not your normal romance," Emily warned.

"I'm all ears."

Emily explained about the ad, about the feeling she had that she was meant to be this man's wife. She opened up about her reservations and wrapped up with how great things were. "I want you guys to meet him."

"Well, that's a no-brainer. We'll shop flights and let you know what's available."

"And I hope we can come out for Thanksgiving or Christmas. We need to talk about the holidays. It would be great if you could meet his parents." She stopped short of saying they were nice people. They weren't bad, but they hadn't welcomed her with open arms. She knew they were resigned to having her in the family, but sharing holidays was questionable. Maybe meeting her parents would soften them even more. Permanency seemed to be the way into their good graces. She had no desire to go anywhere. Everything she'd ever wanted waited for her back home.

She smiled to herself. "Mom, I should go." She suddenly couldn't wait to get home to be with her family. Mom said goodbye and they hung up the phone.

The drive home took for-ev-er. All she could think about was being with her guys again. Hearing Cody laugh or sound out a word. His reading had taken off, and she couldn't wait for him to get back in school and wow his teacher.

Then there was Xavier. Wonderful, sexy, talented Xavier who made her weak in the knees. Once she was through the door, she paused only long enough to listen for Xavier and Cody. She found them in the kitchen, putting the finishing touches on a cracker and cheese tray. Xavier's eyes lit up and warmed at the sight of her.

She went to his side, sliding her arm around him and leaning on his chest. Last night's kiss had thrown open the door, and she was going to sashay right on through and into his arms. The space had been made for her. "What have we got here?"

"A snack," replied Cody. He slid off the barstool and ran around, slamming into their legs. She grunted on impact and then laughed.

Xavier kissed her cheek. "We missed you."

She turned to him. His eyes were full of meaning and caring and so much more. "I can see that," she said, breathless.

He kissed her lightly on the lips, making her knees give out. She sagged into him, wanting so much more than just that small kiss.

Cody sprang back. "Come on." He reached for the heavy wooden tray, almost toppling it in the process.

"Where are we going?" she asked as she steadied it.

"We're going to eat by the pool." His voice was so animated he should have been a cartoon.

"Want to join us?" Xavier traced her cheek.

There were a half dozen to-dos she could have tackled. None of them sounded as good as spending some time with her guys. "I'd love to."

Xavier held her close for a brief moment and then took the tray from Cody. "Will you open the door?"

Cody scampered off to pull on the sliding glass door.

Xavier put his free hand on the small of Emily's back. She didn't think she would ever get enough of his gentle and sweet touches. He knew exactly how to treat her like a lady and make her feel like a woman.

To think that only a couple weeks ago she'd been yearning for this kind of a relationship, and now she had it. Prayers were answered. Romance was real. Love triumphed.

We don't say I love you. Her words came back to her, taunting.

She shoved them away. What were three little words anyway? She didn't have to hear *I love you* to know things were good between them. Her marriage was wonderful. Words were just words.

She stepped through the door and was hit with a blast of chilly wind. "What in the world?" She rubbed at the goose bumps on her arms.

Xavier lifted his chin and sniffed the air. "It smells like a summer storm. They can get dicey."

She nodded but continued to rub her arms. The sudden temperature drop felt like an omen, and her optimism from moments before faltered. They were okay, right? She had a ring on her finger; there was no stronger confirmation that she and Xavier were meant to be together. They were happy. She was happy. She'd contented herself with a loveless marriage and being a mother before; now she had the physical connection she craved.

She should be satisfied; instead, her world was wobbly—like the cheese tray. If she didn't hold it tight, the substance of her marriage would tumble to the ground.

23

XAVIER

$\mathcal{X}$avier glanced around the deli. Emily had mentioned this place a time or two, and he'd wanted to try it out. So when Mark called that morning to see if he could do lunch, he gave him the address.

The room was full of business professionals on their lunch break. He tried to picture Emily in here with the suits and blouses, and he just couldn't. Her clothing would stand out—she would stand out. If he'd come in here one afternoon, not knowing who she was, would he have looked twice? He hoped so. If not, he would have missed out on a beautiful person.

Not that she was unattractive. She was definitely pretty, in a gentle way. He grinned, thinking about the delicate curve of her neck and the softness of her skin.

Mark waved from the counter, and he hurried over to add his order. Once they had their food, they took a seat in the corner. Just as he was about to take a bite of his Reuben, Mark slapped him on the back. "You did it!" He jarred the sandwich loose, and the innards were now outward.

Xavier glared at him. "Did what?"

"Tyson loved 'Love on a Dream.' He wants to buy it, *and* he wants your whole family to fly to Denver to hear it performed for the first time onstage—in two days."

Xavier's scowl evaporated and was replaced with a perma-grin. He'd done it! He sold a song. His first in years. "That's awesome."

"Not only that, he wants to use four more of your songs on his next album. I think this is a comeback for you, man." Mark grabbed his shoulder and pushed him side to side and then let go. He looked at his turkey on rye as if he'd forgotten it was there and he was starving.

"That's the best news." He was shocked and yet relieved and surprised, and yet it was all expected. The kind of music Emily inspired was epic and yet everyday. Falling in love was different for everyone and yet exactly the same. She made it all feel like a dream. Xavier thought of the other songs he had stored away. "I've got more."

"If they're anything like 'Love on a Dream,' I won't have trouble selling them."

"I had a few artists in mind." His old business sense had kicked in, but he hadn't dared bring this up until he had confirmation that he wasn't a hack or a has-been.

Mark laughed. "I'll bet you do."

"But I'd like to work with someone new, someone like Tyson was—is—who will play around with the music." That creative zen they got into made such a difference. Jamming with an artist gave him a chance to get to know their voice in a way that listening to their songs didn't. He could push them to try things and then know if it did or didn't work. That always put him in the flow.

Mark nodded. "I'll start looking for that. You know Tyson gives you credit for his rise to the top."

"He does?" Xavier hadn't heard that before.

"He does to the people who matter. You know how media interviews go. They want to hear about the band and the stage crew—but when you talk to him, the real him, he says your songs were the ones that shot to the top of the weekly top twenty." Mark swiped the mustard off his lips.

Xavier hadn't started putting his sandwich back together, he was so blown away.

"I did some research of my own, and he's right. 'Hard Heart in a Pickup Truck' stayed in the number one spot for three months."

"Why didn't I know this before?"

"Nora." Mark glanced away.

Xavier's curiosity pricked. Mark didn't talk about Nora a lot. He'd let Xavier go on for hours after the funeral, but he never brought her up. "She didn't pass for a year after 'Hard Heart' was released. What did that have to do with the song's success?"

Mark set his sandwich down and wiped his fingers with a paper napkin. "I didn't want to ever tell you, but I think you need to know. She asked me not to talk about how well your songs did after you sold them. She said she didn't want you to let the success go to your head, for you to think you were big time."

Xavier shoved the plate away from him. He didn't quite believe Mark. Then again, Mark didn't have a reason to lie. "Why would she do that?"

"She said that once you started feeling the pressure of a hit song, your music would suffer. I think she was trying to protect you."

He shook his head sadly. That sounded like something Nora would say. She was all about art for the sake of art—not money. There was one song she'd insisted he never pitch because it was too *special*. He'd bought into it then, but now he wondered. Another thought came to mind, one that he'd never expressed but that had stayed with him from early on. "Mark, do you think Nora was jealous of my success?" He felt bad even saying the words out loud. Nora had been a cellist, a good one. She'd tried out for several symphonies but never got a call back. Then she was pregnant and she packed away her cello.

Mark tipped his head from side to side. "I think she felt like you were above country music, that you should have stuck with the poetry you were doing when you two met."

"I only did that as a class assignment."

"Right, but it was what she liked. Commercializing lyrics bothered her."

"I know." Xavier grabbed a napkin and began folding it into a tiny square. Much like he'd felt being married to Nora. "*I* love it, though. I love hearing my songs on the radio and seeing them performed onstage." He threw the square aside. "If I had half of Tyson's stage presence, I'd be up there myself." Stage presence? More like less of his own stage fright. His hands felt like clubs up there, and it made playing a guitar impossible.

Mark smiled. "I think you could go for it. Especially if you were singing one of Emily's songs."

Xavier lowered his brow in confusion. "Emily's songs?"

"That's what I've named this new batch of music. You wrote it for Emily, didn't you? Or I should say because of her. I'm so glad you guys fell in love. It was unexpected, but it's great."

"Love?" Xavier scoffed. "Don't get me wrong, I like her—a lot. But love? That's not really possible."

Mark gave him a do-you-think-I'm-stupid look. "It's in your music, man. It's like she opened your heart and pulled the notes out."

Xavier pushed back from the table, agitated. "What Emily did was bring order to my life. She makes healthy meals that feed my brain and body and son. She cares for Cody so I'm not constantly worried about him. She hasn't unlocked anything."

"Okay." Mark held up his hands. "I surrender. You're not in love with her."

"Thank you." Xavier grabbed his plate back and popped a piece of meat into his mouth.

"But can I just ask … why not?"

He chewed. "Because I don't need a distraction, and that's what love is. It's work and effort, and it takes so much time to keep the other person happy. You have to constantly monitor your relationship and make sure you're putting enough of yourself into it while keeping some back to survive. Love is … exhausting."

Mark stared at him as he slowly reached for another napkin. "That's telling."

Xavier stood. "I think I'll take this to go." He marched out of the deli without getting a box to wrap his sandwich. He didn't even care. He set the plate on the seat of his SUV.

He wasn't in love with Emily. He couldn't afford to be. The whole reason he'd picked her was because he knew he wouldn't fall in love with her. He didn't have time to fall in love. He had a comeback to make and songs to write. Things were finally looking up for him.

He could kiss her. Laugh with her. Raise Cody. But love her? That was out of the question.

Then why was everybody asking him about it?

First his mom and now Mark.

He shook his head. They must be reading things into the situation. They hadn't had their conversation where he'd told her he liked her—didn't have to. They didn't need words. They had expressed themselves with touch. That was enough for the both of them.

24

EMILY

*E*mily bit her lip as she stared at the little black dress she'd packed to wear to the Tyson concert. The black lace across the sweetheart bodice was a little on the risqué side compared to what she'd been wearing, but it was conservative when compared to her high school prom dress. A couple months ago, she wouldn't have blinked before putting this on; now she blushed thinking of how Xavier was going to react.

"You're going to look so hot." Lexi fanned her face as she came into the room.

"That's what I'm afraid of."

Tyson had rented them a four-bedroom suite. She and Xavier decided to invite Lexi along to watch Cody. She got to go to a free concert and trip to Denver, and Cody would be well taken care of while she and Xavier schmoozed with the bigwigs.

"What? You're scared Xavier won't be able to control himself after seeing you in that dress?"

"No, I'm afraid he *will* be able to control himself after seeing me in the dress." She crossed her arms. "He hasn't kissed me in days, and I'm going through withdrawals."

Lexi laughed. "Don't worry. We'll get you all done up, and he'll lose his ability to think rationally."

"Stop! You make him sound like a cartoon coyote."

"Sweetie, inside all men are cartoon coyotes. Some are just better at hiding it than others."

Emily laughed. "Let's get this hair done." She pulled out the high bun and let the waves tumble around her shoulders.

Lexi added some shine spray and mused the waves. "Boom! Sexy bedhead done."

Emily had to admit, having her hair loose again felt freeing. She changed into the dress, and Lexi did a smoky eye, adding false lashes that made her blue eyes pop. She sighed happily. "It's more than I used to do, but I've missed wearing eye shadow." She spun around. "I feel like me again."

Lexi patted her arm. "You look beautiful. Now go get your man. He's in Cody's room."

"Thanks."

"Thank *you*! That autographed picture of Tyson is payment enough. I can't believe he was at your house and you didn't text me to come right over. What is the point of being sisters if we don't have each other's back?"

Emily laughed as she hurried out of the room. She wished she could set Lexi and Tyson up—she had a feeling they would get along. She just had to figure out the right time and place to ask him. There was no need to ask Lexi. She'd cancel surgery to be there. Now that Emily knew Tyson was a good man under all the spotlights and album covers, she was working on a plan.

But her plan tonight was to blow Xavier's socks off.

She tapped on Cody's open door and walked in.

Xavier and Cody were on the bed, reading. Xavier's black cowboy boots dangled off the side like he was afraid to get them on the coverlet. She smiled. They were as shiny as if he'd bought them yesterday but scuffed in all the right places. His faded jeans were long enough to stack on his boots. He wore a button-up shirt and a belt buckle that Tyson had given him long ago. He had three-day scruff but had shaved his neck and sculpted the rest. He was so hot, he could melt lava.

Cody was dressed just like his dad. The two of them together were so cute she could hardly stand it.

"Does anybody want to go to a concert?" She lifted a hand in question.

They looked up, and Xavier's eyes popped. She laughed inside, thinking of her conversation with Lexi. *Coyote.*

He slowly got off the bed, his eyes never leaving her, like he was afraid that if he blinked, she'd evaporate. "Your hair," he whispered.

She ran her hand over the waves. "I think it grew two inches in the last month." It probably had, since she hadn't used heat on it.

He came to her and lifted a strand, rubbing it between his thumb and fingers. "It's so soft."

She cut off the diatribe about conditioning treatments and a list of the products she applied to get that "natural" soft feeling before it came out of her mouth. "Thanks," she whispered.

He let her hair fall to her shoulder and moved his hand to her neck, his thumb just over the pulse in her collarbone. Her heart pounded, and she wondered if he could hear it. His pupils were big, and she had a hard time catching her breath.

"Dad!" Cody tugged at Xavier's arm. "Let's go."

Emily released the air in her lungs and turned her attention to Cody. It felt safer that way. If she continued to take in Xavier's intensity, she'd melt. "Are you sure you're ready?" she asked Cody.

He glanced down at his own pair of boots. "Yep."

She grinned. Oh, how she loved this little guy. Bending over, she swooped him into a hug.

"Hey! Cowboys don't hug," he complained.

"They hug pretty girls every chance they get." Xavier wrapped his arms around both of them.

Emily's heart opened up and swirled around the two of them. She was so full of love for these two, for her family, that she didn't ever want to let go. Cody squirmed, letting her know she'd reached her hugging limit. "All right, I guess we're off to a concert."

As excited as she was to hear Xavier's song performed by Tyson, she would have stayed in that moment forever.

25

XAVIER

*T*he noise at a concert could cause hearing damage, and Tyson's concerts were known to be particularly loud because of all the screaming women.

Xavier had told Mark that he'd be the one onstage if he had half Tyson's stage presence. He took in the women waving their hands, swooning, dancing, and yelling, and decided he'd rather have the quiet life of a songwriter, a father, and mostly a husband. He didn't want all these women; he just wanted Emily.

The opening strains of his song started, and he put his arm around Emily, pulling her close.

She. Was. Breathtaking.

He'd always known she had a shape under those baggy clothes. He'd seen hints of it here and there. He just never put much thought into what she would look like in a skintight dress. As far as dresses went, this one was conservative. He'd seen women wear less to the grocery store. Then again, he hadn't kissed those women, hadn't held them close, hadn't shared his days and thoughts and hopes with them. Those women didn't champion his music or tenderly hug his son. It wasn't just the dress that made Emily so beautiful—it was Emily's goodness. She was a good person through and through.

He moved his hand from her back to her hip. She smiled up at him and snuggled into his side, her hand on his chest. Tyson stepped to the microphone, the lights dimmed, and the music that had flown through him to the strings of a guitar filled the stadium.

"Unexpected, you were unexpected." Tyson's deep voice did more with the words than Xavier's tenor. He sang along anyway, close to Emily, wanting to share the words with her, the meaning.

"But when you came into my life, a light went on, you were so bright."

Emily began to sway, as if she were so caught up in the notes and the guitar and the single fiddle dancing slowly in the background.

"And now I know I can't live without you, girl. You are my world."

Xavier's phone buzzed in his pocket. He ignored it. If it was about Cody, Lexi would have called Emily. Everything and everyone else could wait. He was captured in the experience of watching Emily while his music played. Her eyes closed and her face relaxed. She hummed a few notes, and he couldn't hold back. He leaned in and kissed her as the music swelled, his heart, mind, and soul building right along with it.

His phone buzzed again. He continued to ignore it; kissing Emily was worth a missed call. He wouldn't be able to hear in this place anyway, especially with the women crying and swooning. It created a sense that they were in their own bubble of time and space. In fact, time had taken on a ¾ beat. As the song came to a close, he pressed his forehead to hers and took a deep breath of her vanilla concoction.

The concert ended three songs later. The crowed screamed for an encore. "He'll never come back out!" Xavier yelled near Emily's ear. Not so romantic, but necessary. "Let's get out of here."

Emily pulled out her phone. "Lexi says she and Cody are already back at the hotel. They left before the last song was over. He was falling asleep in his headphones."

Xavier had bought him noise-cancelling headphones. He'd seen several other children with them as well.

He checked Insta and found it blowing up about his song. The fans loved it. All of them.

As they were leaving the building, his phone rang. He glanced at the screen, seeing Mark's name he answered. "Hey, man. That was amazing. Tyson did right by the music. I couldn't have asked for a better representation." He held fast to Emily with his spare hand, lacing their fingers together. A quiet dinner awaited them at a nice bistro two blocks away. They'd walk, giving the after-concert traffic a chance to clear out.

"Where were you?" Mark yelled. The sound of the stage crew packing up came through the line.

"I was at the concert. Great tickets, by the way." He winked at Emily and plunged through a group of twenty.

"Why didn't you answer the phone?"

"I—what is going on?" Mark never drilled him like this.

"I had Todd Maxwell backstage. He heard the song and wanted to talk to you about buying a set for Sunlight Records."

"That's great!" Xavier threw his and Emily's hands in the air. Everything was coming up roses for them. They had a beautiful son. Tyson just played his new hit song. He kissed the most beautiful woman on the planet. A contract with Sunlight Records would set them up for life.

"No. It's not great. He had to leave, and the offer expired with him."

"How?"

"He said if he couldn't get a hold of you, he didn't want to work with you."

A feeling of falling off a cliff swept through his stomach. "That's ridiculous." Even as he complained, he knew that was how Maxwell worked. He demanded his people be there when he was ready for them, not the other way around. "What can I do?"

"Answer your phone!" There was a pause. "Look, man, we needed that contract. Both of us."

"I know. I'm sorry." He dropped Emily's hand and tugged at his hair. "We'll figure something out." They said goodbye and hung up. Xavier mimed throwing his phone at the brick wall. He'd screwed up —big time. His comeback was falling apart right in front of him.

"What's the matter?" Emily asked.

He looked at her, in her stunning dress, her hair framing her beautiful face, and he realized what she'd done to him. She'd become a distraction. The very distraction he was looking to avoid. She'd helped him write again and she'd wooed Tyson back into his life, but when it came down to it, she'd drawn him in to a web of attraction and desire that had stepped in front of the comeback career path he'd started out on. "You distracted me."

She fluttered her lashes. "I did what?"

He took a step away from her, as if she had tractor beams for eyes and would draw him right back in if he let her. "I ignored an important call because I was more worried about you than I was about my career." He shook his head as if he could shake loose of the thoughts telling him to shut up. They wanted him to stop making her look like he was tearing her heart to pieces.

"Xavier, I'm not sure what I did."

"It was me." He thrust his fist at his chest, pounding hard. "I set up boundaries when we got married, and I've crossed them." He tucked his phone in his pocket and tugged on his shirt sleeves. "It won't happen again." He strode toward the bistro.

"Wait a second." She grabbed his hand to stop him, and he yanked it away like she'd scalded his skin. She jerked in surprise. "*What* won't happen again?"

"The physical contact, the kissing …" He ticked them off on his fingers. "Slow dancing. All of it."

She stared at him, her face unreadable. "Like—never again?"

"Never," he responded, slicing his hand through the air to accentuate his determination.

She pinched the bridge of her nose. "I'm not sure I'm okay with that."

He coughed in surprise. Did she not hear him? She'd distracted him from the most important meeting of his life. He couldn't concentrate when she was around. He wasn't made to be a lover and a businessman. Those were two separate skill sets. When he was flooded with desire, he didn't think rationally. "You agreed happily when we got married."

"Right." She glanced down at her fingers twisted in front of her. "But that was before I knew this kind of love was possible. It's easy to agree to miss something when you've never had it."

"Well, I did have it before, and it's not all it's cracked up to be. We're better off without it." He walked seven steps before he realized she wasn't with him. He spun around to see her standing in the same place he'd left her, tears streaming down her cheeks. He stared in awe. She was beautiful and broken. *Shoot!* A sad, lonely song began to play in his head.

"I can't go back, Xavier. I can't go back to the emptiness we called a marriage before."

"Well, I can't live falling all over you all day long. I have a job to do. One that I've left undone for too long."

She sucked in. A swarm of emotions battled in her eyes. She loved him, and the fierceness of it was enough to stab him. He'd not seen it before, not put a name to it because he couldn't look further than himself. "Then I have to go."

His heart cracked. Go? She couldn't go. They were married. She loved him. He—he had deep feelings for her. "What about Cody?" he asked, though his real question was *What about me?* Wasn't he enough to stick around for? Wasn't what they shared big enough for her?

She shook her head. "Tell him I love him." She gasped and spun away, running, dodging between people who turned to stare after her.

"What about me?" he asked softly, feeling abandoned and lost. He glanced down at his hands as if he could see the pride he'd held on to so tightly. They were empty. "I made the right choice." He made his hands into fists. "I chose supporting my son. If she can't put that first, then it wasn't meant to be."

As they so often did, his thoughts grabbed on to the phrase *wasn't meant to be.* Usually that meant a melody followed, but there was no music on that crowded street. He stuffed his hands in his pockets, hunched his shoulders, and made his way slowly to the hotel. Maybe Emily was there and they could talk things through. He'd been hasty and argumentative and accusing. They'd had disagreements before, and they'd worked them out. This would be no different.

But when he got to the hotel, her room was empty. Cody slept peacefully in his bed. Emily's door was shut, and there wasn't any sound on the other side when he pressed his ear to the wood.

When he woke up in the morning, Emily was gone. The suite was empty of all girly things.

The music was silent.

26

EMILY

*E*mily left the witness stand, her hands shaking and her cheeks soaked with sorrow and fear. She wore a pair of black slacks and a silky blouse—something she hadn't worn since she'd married Xavier. The clothes felt good, like she'd picked up a piece of herself once again.

Roger winked at her as she passed him sitting at the defendant's table with his highly polished and gelled attorney.

She took a seat next to her sister on the bench on the other side of the room, where he was barely in her peripheral vision. She didn't want to take her eyes off of him—she wouldn't look away from a snake on the hiking trail—but seeing him again brought back the whole experience.

She wished Xavier were with her. Having his arm protectively wrapped around her shoulder would calm the storm raging in her stomach. She hadn't eaten much over the last week—not since she'd left Colorado the night of the concert. Her tears continued to flow as she listened to closing arguments.

The judge was quick with his gavel. Guilty. Three years imprisonment with the possibility of early parole and counseling.

"Mrs. Cohen." The judge looked over his glasses and found her in the sea of faces. "I suggest you find yourself a good counselor. Today was a difficult day, and having someone to talk to will help."

She nodded. She still had the number from the woman she'd seen just after the attack. "I will. Thank you."

Lexi turned her away from Roger as he was led out of the courtroom to be fitted for an orange jumpsuit. "These tears aren't just for today, are they?"

Emily sniffed and searched through her purse for a tissue. "I can't stop crying."

"He's a jerk, sweetie. You need to forget him." Lexi rubbed her arm.

"I wish I could. It was so wonderful. I'd had to give up a part of me."

"The flirty, fun part full of joy?"

"Not all of it. But the part of me that enjoyed feeling pretty. It was so dumb that I couldn't wear makeup or leave my hair down."

"I don't think that was because of Xavier. I think that was a shield you put up because of what happened at work." Lexi offered her knowledge in a quiet and contemplative way.

Emily nodded. "Xavier got through the shield, though. It wasn't a very good one."

"Well, it was made of cotton." Lexi bumped her.

She ran her fingers through her silky tresses. She hadn't pulled it back in days. "My body was part of my identity—especially because I used it to teach yoga. I missed that too." She hugged herself. "Being Cody's mom was amazing. I loved it so much—I just wish there was a way I could have been me and mom."

The room began to shift as another case was brought before the judge. Lexi lead Emily out the back doors, through the hallway, and into the sunlight. "Xavier is an idiot for not valuing what he had when he had it."

Emily glanced down at her ring. "We're still married," she hedged.

Lexi stopped their progress with a tug. "Do you want to go back in and file for an annulment?"

Emily stared up at the imposing courthouse with its leaf-topped pillars and scales of justice carved in marble. "I'd rather not go back in there right now." She clasped her hands together in front of her. It wasn't just facing the courthouse again that weighed on her. She wasn't ready to say goodbye to Xavier and Cody and the time they'd spent together. Closure on the attack was a blessing, a sweetness she was happy to grasp on to and carry throughout her life.

Her marriage was sweet too. At least for a time. And she wanted to hold that for as long as she could. Removing the ring on her left hand or signing papers to dissolve the union was overwhelming. Being the one to cut ties made her mouth sour. She clutched her left hand to her chest. "I want to be a Mrs. for a while longer."

Lexi nodded, her lips sealed shut.

Emily climbed into the car and watched the courthouse fade in the side mirror. She wanted to hold her guys and be held. Her arms were empty without them.

27

XAVIER

*X*avier reached for the phone with his right hand. His left arm was wrapped around Cody, who was screaming and kicking his legs because he wanted to ride his bike and Xavier had said no.

His mom came in from the other room and took Cody. "Come here, sweet boy."

Xavier raised his eyebrows. Only a grandmother could call a tantrum-throwing child *sweet*. He and Cody had been out of sorts since they had come home from the concert. "Sorry. He's adjusting to not having Emily around."

"Just about as well as his father, I'd say." She headed to the kitchen with a stern set to her brow that wasn't directed at the panting child in her arms.

Xavier answered the phone call with a curt "Hello."

"Mr. Cohen?"

"This is he."

"This is Jennifer from Dr. Obrien's office. We have the results back from Cody's blood work yesterday."

Xavier reached for the couch, needing to hold on to something. He'd taken Cody in for a follow-up appointment on his prediabetes. This could be the moment he found out that his son was diabetic and their worlds changed forever. They were already going through a huge transition with Emily gone; they didn't need any more of an upheaval in their lives.

"Yes?" He swallowed thickly. Emily should be here for this. She should be holding his hand and holding him up. Strike that—he should be holding her. She'd put so much effort into meal planning and helping Cody become more active; she had her heart and soul in that kid. She should be here, and he'd chased her away.

"The tests came back normal."

"What does that mean?" Normal for prediabetic children, or *normal* normal?

"It means Cody is out of the danger zone. Dr. Obrien recommends you continue with the changes in his diet, and we'd like him to come back in 3 months for a hemoglobin a1-C."

Xavier fell against the couch. "Thank you." He breathed the words, unable to take a full breath.

The nurse wished him a good day and said goodbye. Xavier stared at his phone, feeling like he was in a dream. He lifted his head, looking for Emily to share the good news, but suddenly realized she wasn't there. He groaned.

Mom came back in. "What's the matter?"

"That was Cody's doc. He's in the clear."

She put her hands on her hips. "You should tell your face this is a happy thing."

"I know. I was just going to tell Emily, but ..." He shoved his phone into his pocket. The weight of her absence was too much to bear. "You should have seen her face. I think I broke her heart—no, *shattered* it. I can't stop thinking about what she said about how she couldn't go back once she knew how good it could be. I'd opened my heart and then slammed the door on her fingers. What is wrong with me?"

His mom crossed the room and took his face in her hands. "Oh, honey. You fell hard for that girl. You have to tell her how you feel."

He blinked. "I thought you didn't like her."

Mom gave him an apologetic smile. "I didn't think she was authentic. But now I wonder if the problem wasn't you all along."

"Thanks, *Mom*."

"You have to admit, you've been emotionally unavailable since Nora passed away. You've been living but not thriving, coping but not caring. It's like you took a step back from everyone so that you wouldn't get hurt. I get it. Losing someone you love takes a toll. But hon, you've got to step back into the place where you love without fear."

"I'm not sure I can. What if I love Emily, give my whole heart over to her, and I lose her too?"

"One: You already love her." She gave him a look that said he'd better not argue. He didn't want to; he yearned to break out and sing the words *I Love You* to Em. "Two: There are no guarantees in this life. Even if you have Emily, there will be heartache and pain—no marriage gets by without it. But I can promise you that if you grab the good times when you have them, the hard times are easier."

The truth of his mother's word sank deep into his mind. The last couple of months hadn't been easy. He'd been under a lot of stress from the comeback and with Cody's health. Yet they felt like the best months of his life. "I need to get her back."

Mom winked. "What are you waiting for?"

He grinned. "Can you watch Cody?" he asked as he headed to the shower. It had been 36 hours, and he wasn't about to show up on Emily's doorstep smelling like he'd been dragged through a cow field and slept in a barn.

"I'll plan to stay the night. You go do what you gotta do."

In his bedroom, he yanked his shirt over his head and started the shower. As the steam built up, a melody filled his mind. He didn't need to write it down; the notes were written on his heart.

28

*E*mily pulled a fuzzy blanket over her legs and sipped cocoa. Yes, it was August, but she needed comfort. Which was why she was wrapped up like a snow bunny and watching a Hallmark Christmas movie.

Lexi came through the door with a bag of groceries strung over one arm. She frowned. "Hallmark? Again?"

Emily frowned. "I need a happily ever after tonight."

Lexi sighed. "Then you might as well go outside."

Emily wrinkled her forehead in confusion. Lexi waved her out, setting down the groceries and following her onto the porch. "I don't see anything."

Lexi put her finger over her mouth. "Listen."

At first, Emily didn't hear anything. Then, the sound of an acoustic guitar playing the first notes of "Can't Help Falling in Love" drifted through the complex. "What in the world?" Emily followed the sound around the building to the common area with a playground and a few picnic tables.

In the middle of the park was Xavier, his guitar over his shoulder, his hands shaking as he strummed. "Wise men say …" he sang.

Neighbors had gathered. He glanced around uneasily as more poured from their homes to watch.

Emily brought her hands to her mouth in shock. Xavier said he had stage fright, but now she could see the results of it: the moisture beading on his forehead, his voice warbling, and his knees shaking with such force that she had no idea how he stayed upright.

"… but I can't help …" He strummed cords, making the break between verses longer as he worked his mouth as if it had gone dry. He hadn't seen her yet, but he continued on. "… falling in love with you."

She whimpered into her hands, and his gaze zeroed in on her. He stood taller, his voice growing stronger. He began to walk toward her, and her feet moved toward him. He sang slower than Elvis, drawing out the notes in an achy plea for her love.

"… Some things are meant to be …" he crooned. His stage fright was still there, but as he sang, he sang just for her.

She was taken back to the day in his studio when they'd teased about music and Elvis. That was the first time they'd flirted. The first time she'd thought she might have found her dreams and hopes for a forever family.

"… Take my whole heart too …"

She nodded.

He strummed as he spoke, his hands moving with ease. "I'm a fool, Emily. I didn't see the jewel I had. I didn't look in my own heart to see how much I love you until you were gone. For that, and everything else I've ever done that made you feel less than a goddess, I apologize."

His words washed over her like a bath of hot cocoa and a million Hallmark movies. She threw her arms around his neck, the guitar strings pressing into her belly and the music stopping—except she could hear it still echoing in her head and in her heart. "Say it again?" she asked.

"I love you. I love you. I love you." He wrapped his arms around her and lifted her off the ground.

She laughed at his exuberance.

He set her down, gently, but didn't loosen his hold. His eyes dipped to her lips. "Please come home, Emily."

She didn't answer, except to raise up on her toes and press her lips to his. His arms were strong, his kisses sure. A moment later, she pulled back, running her hands over his shoulders. "This is my home."

His cheeks crinkled with a smile that melted her heart. "And you're my music." He tucked his guitar behind his back, and there was nothing left between them but the love they shared.

EPILOGUE

XAVIER

*X*avier entered the kitchen to a familiar sight. He took a deep breath, grateful for what the last three months had brought into his life.

Emily was at the counter, chopping vegetables for a salad. Cody sat on a barstool, peeling carrots and chattering away. They giggled over something he'd missed because he was too busy staring at the perfection before him. The only thing that would make it better was if he had his arms around Emily.

He wandered in and took up a place behind her, wrapping his arms around her middle and burying his face in her neck. She'd worn her hair up tonight, and her perfume enveloped his senses in joy.

"I can't chop with you trying to seduce me." She bumped him with her hip, doing nothing to create space.

Since tonight was her night and not a night he could whisk her off to the deck for kisses and cocoa, he relaxed his hold. "Who are these people again?" He snatched a carrot from Cody's cutting board, earning a glare from his son. Emily was as relieved as he had been to hear Cody's prognosis. They still had to watch him for signs of diabetes, but they were hopeful.

"One of my yoga students and her husband. You'll love them." She giggled, making him a little worried about who exactly she'd invited to dinner.

Emily had picked up teaching a couple classes a week. She'd told him about the attack, and they'd talked over the pros and cons of her returning to work there—with her deciding she'd rather have less stress than a PT position but still help people feel good in their bodies.

The counselor had helped her work through the trauma of facing Roger in court. She was determined not to let him steal her happiness, and she enjoyed teaching yoga. Cody worked his schedule around hers. She'd blossomed even more since her return. At least once a day, he thanked his lucky stars that he'd married such an amazing woman.

Mark yelled hello from the front door. It didn't matter that Xavier and Emily were living like newlyweds these days; he still didn't knock.

"We're back here," Emily called.

Xavier loved the way his best friend and his wife had gelled. Emily was all about making their family bigger and having their home open and welcoming. She made people feel important.

Mark came in, his hand on the small of his date's back. He introduced her as Jenni, and everyone said hello. Emily offered them a tray of cheese and crackers.

The doorbell rang. Emily glanced at the clock, "I'll get it." She hurried to remove her apron and darted for the entryway.

Mark placed a piece of provolone on a cracker. "Do you know these guys?"

Xavier shook his head.

"It's so wonderful you could make it." Emily's voice proceeded her into the room. She entered, a funny smile on her face. "And this is my family." She moved to the side to reveal a smaller woman with gray hair and a large smile. Behind her stood Mr. Maxwell, owner of Sunlight Records.

Mark dropped the cracker and cheese and his jaw.

Emily introduced Mark to the man who had the power to crush his career. "And you know Mark Johnson. This is his lovely date, Jenni."

Stunned, Xavier blurted the first thing that came to mind as he pumped the man's hand. "I had no idea you lived in Moose Creek."

He laughed. "My wife grew up here. I couldn't get her to leave if I promised her a private island."

Mrs. Maxwell elbowed him. "You did, remember?" She wore a pair of leopard-print leggings and a black shirt that hung off one shoulder.

His eyes twinkled. "And you said no."

She shook her head. "I love my mountains."

"How ...?" Mark stumbled turning to Emily. "How do you know them?"

Mr. Maxwell chuckled, answering for her. "It was the video."

Xavier's face burned. "I'm never going to live that down." Someone had filmed him singing in the park for Emily and posted it on the city web page.

His wife stepped in. "I told him I knew Emily. I took her yoga class at the PT center in town. He asked to meet you, so I invited us over for dinner." She cupped her hand around her mouth. "I don't cook."

"I like working with people who have their priorities straight." Maxwell's eyes fell on Cody, who slipped his hand in Xavier's. "You've got a lovely family. Let's set up a time to go over what you've got."

Xavier's head spun with the possibilities. "I-I'd like that."

"He'd love it," threw out Mark, making them all laugh.

Xavier put his arm around Emily. Tonight was her night—even if she'd done this for him. "But tonight's not about business. Emily's made something delicious." He kissed her temple and whispered, "Thank you."

She shrugged—like it was no big deal to get a studio owner to come to dinner. "It's a night for announcements too."

Xavier glanced at Mark. Just how close where he and Jenni? "Yeah?"

"What announcement?" asked Mark. If he was trying to throw them off, he wasn't very good at it.

"I think Cody has something to say." She ruffled his hair, and he looked up at her with a grin bigger than the sunrise.

"Now?" he asked.

"Now," she confirmed.

He threw his arms open and shouted, "I'm going to be a big brother!"

Xavier's arms went numb.

Mark hooted. Jenni clapped. Mr. and Mrs. Maxwell whooped and hugged.

Emily turned to put her hands on Xavier's chest. She tipped her chin up and gazed into his eyes. "You look a little surprised."

He brushed his hand over her cheek. "A lot."

She giggled. Her cheeks turned pink.

He smiled and kissed her once and then once again. "I hope it's a girl and she's as beautiful as you."

"I want a brother." Cody folded his arms and pouted, making the adults laugh.

Emily kissed Xavier once more. "If not, we can always try again."

He liked the sound of that. Once he'd opened his heart to Emily, he found that there was so much room inside of him to love—more than he'd ever thought possible. And when he gave it to her, it came back to him tenfold. He'd forever be in her debt. And he hoped that never changed.

WANT to read more arranged marriage stories? How about arranging matches for billionaires? :)

Check out the first book in the Billionaire Marriage Brokers series.

The Academic Bride
Available on Amazon

CLAIM YOUR FREE BOOK TODAY!

An *It Could Happen to You* retelling with a twist!

This story is an irresistible contemporary romance about a not-so-humble cop who splits his raffle ticket with an unlucky waitress and the actor who falls in love with her.

You'll also be registered for Lucy's newsletter where you'll receive free delicious recipes and updates about her book releases.

Go to:
https://mybookcave.com/d/c7300449/
to receive your FREE gift.

NOW AVAILABLE FROM BESTSELLING AND AWARD-WINNING AUTHOR LUCY MCCONNELL

Read on to discover more sweet romances from
bestselling author Lucy McConnell.

Billionaire Marriage Brokers

The Academic Bride
The Organized Bride
The Professional Bride
The Country Bride
The Protective Groom
The Resilient Bride
The Athletic Groom
The Corporate Groom

Marrying Miss Kringle
Ginger
Lux
Frost
Robyn

Fake Fiancee For Christmas
His Wedding Date Fake Fiancee
Her Totally Hot Forbidden Fake Fiance

MyHeartChannel Romances
EverDayLove!
The Great Christmas Contest
Christmas Magic

Billionaire Bachelor Cove
Her Beast of a Billionaire Boss
Her Awkward Blind Date with the Billionaire
Her Marriage Pact with the Billionaire

Dating Mr. Baseball
Delay of Game
Caught Looking
Intentional Walk
Heavy Hitter

Texas Titans Romances
The Miracle Groom
The Warrior Groom
The Guardian Groom
The Devout Groom

Or get all four football romances at a great price and FREE on KU

Lucy's Football Collection

The Snow Valley Series

Welcome to Snow Valley, Montana, where romance is always in season.
Blue Christmas

Love in Light and Shadow
Romancing Her Husband
Wedding Fever
One Date Deal
His Wedding Date Fake Fiancee

Echo Ridge Romances
For a small town in Up-state New York, Echo Ridge has a great
big heart.

The Candy Counter Heiress
The Lion, the Witch, and the Library
A Brand New Second Chance
While You Were Skiing
A Brandnew Ball Game

Or, get all four books at an amazing price and FREE on KU
Echo Ridge Romance Collection

The Destination Billionaire Romance Series
Beautiful locations, handsome heroes, and romance.

The Reclusive Billionaire
Royal Distraction

Collections
Great for binge reading!

Sports Romance Collection
Billionaire Romance Series Sampler
Billionaire Marriage Brokers Brides Collection

ABOUT THE AUTHOR

Lucy McConnell has always been a reader and a writer. She writes fantasy, clean romance, Christian romance, historical fiction, and cookbooks under the name Christina Dymock.

When she's not writing, you can find her volunteering at the elementary school or the church; shuttling kids to baseball, soccer, basketball, or rodeo, depending on the time of year; skiing with her family; wake boarding; cycling; or curled up with a good book.

You can sign up for her newsletter by clicking here and can check out here website here: http://lucymcconnell.wordpress.com/